With compliments to

*Eddy, my husband,*

*and my Chihuahuas*
*Poppy and Didi,*

*who never miss a line.*

# The Windamere Series

*Set against the enduring landscapes of rural Australia, The Windamere Series follows the lives, loves, and legacies of families shaped by land, loyalty, and quiet resilience.*

*Each novel stands alone, while together they form a generational story of change, belonging, and the bonds that endure across time.*

*Windamere's Rose is the opening novel in the series.*

# CHAPTER 1 - NURSE ASHFORD

## Historical Notes

During World War II, Alexandra Military Hospital provided care for injured soldiers. Its red brick structure, arched windows, and well-kept gardens reflected the era's architecture, while the sight of military vehicles and personnel emphasised its critical role during wartime.

'Rose, come over here,' Sue called, her voice tinged with urgency yet gentle as a breeze, beckoning her towards one of the new casualties.

With deliberate care, Rose completed the dressing on her current patient. She tenderly patted his shoulder and adjusted the surrounding blanket, ensuring he was warm and comfortable. The soldier's weary eyes softened, taking solace in her radiant smile, a beacon of light in the hospital's harrowing darkness. She had a unique way of making each one feel irreplaceable, a jewel amidst the rubble of war. For Rose, every patient was a friend—each recovery a silent triumph, and each loss a deep, wrenching sorrow that lingered like an unhealed wound in her heart.

Peering down at Sue's patient sprawled on his stomach, the sharp tang of antiseptic mingling assaulted Rose's senses with the spicy scent of the cream, yet neither could fully mask the disgusting odour of burnt flesh. The acrid smell alone painted a vivid picture of the severity of his burns. Infection, the relentless tormentor of soldiers, hovered like a dark cloud over his precarious fate.

'Get closer and listen,' Sue said, moving aside to let Rose lean in and catch the faint murmurings. Urgency filled her voice, and worry etched the lines on her face. 'Doesn't it sound like Windermere? Isn't that where you're from?'

Rose bent lower, her ears straining to catch each barely audible word. There it was.

'Windamere, Windamere, Windamere,' he repeatedly whispered as a chant anchored in desperation, as if clinging to the name could somehow pull him through.

'Yes, it's Windermere,' Rose confirmed, eyes scanning his sun-darkened face. Deep etchings of pain marked his expression. His brows furrowed intensely over tightly shut eyes, every muscle tensed in a battle for life. Each whispered word was a lifeline. 'But I don't recognise him.'

'His name is Rory Anderson. Does that ring a bell?' Sue inquired, her brow furrowing as she leaned over the bed.

Rose paused, a puzzled expression crossing her face as she tried to dig through her memory. 'No, afraid not,' she finally replied, shaking her head. The name could have been anyone, a ghost from the past or a stranger she had never met. Sue's persistence only added to the mystery surrounding this elusive Rory.

'Pity he's dark and handsome, just my type,' Sue quipped with a light-hearted laugh, though her eyes betrayed a flicker of concern. 'I was hoping for an introduction when he comes to.'

'His burns are severe,' Rose replied somberly, her gaze sombre. 'He will need to fight to survive,' she murmured, almost to herself.

That indomitable will sometimes carves a path between life and death. She resolved to visit him tomorrow, reflecting on the familiar towns scattered throughout the Windermere district. Did he come from one of them?

Calm washed over her as she replaced the blood-soaked dressing, lost in the thought of 'Windamere.' Each whisper of the name reminded her of peace, but the chaos of the ward was an ever-present truth.

The ward was a cacophony of suffering, filled with soldiers in various stages of agony. The air was thick with the nauseating stench of burnt flesh mingling with the clammy scent of impending death, evolving the space into a harrowing purgatory for nurses. Still, Rose pressed on, her steps heavy but filled with an unyielding resolve.

Every inhale brought a stinging awareness of the possibility of another life slipping away under her care. 'Someone has to fight for those who have fought their last on the battlefield,' she reminded herself, her voice barely a whisper over the relentless sounds of anguish.

Each soldier she rescued delivered a brief yet potent rush of euphoria, a fleeting glimmer that life might conquer after all. However, every passing soul gnawed a piece of their spirit away, leaving behind the sad recognition that soon enough, another would occupy the vacant bed. The vicious cycle of hope and despair perpetually renewed itself, tinged with the scents, sounds, and weight of suffering that enveloped every corner of the ward.

Rose thought of her cherished Windermere with a glimmer in her eyes. It was not just Windermere's haunting beauty that drew her in, but her family as well.

There in the graveyard lay her parents at rest, where the crisp air carried the fragrance of damp earth and blossoming wildflowers. The serenity, the rich green of the surrounding hills, and the occasional bird song create a symphony of nature that enchants all who visit. That they had a last resting place comforted her.

She pondered what made his Windermere so special, wondering what could drive him to such lengths, its importance profound enough to spur his relentless fight. Who was he? It puzzled her why he lingered in her thoughts after, little more than a whisper in the cacophony of her troubled mind. Yet, he stood out against the backdrop of chaos, an enigma wrapped in the folds of her uncertain emotions.

Drained from another punishing shift, she collapsed onto her bed. The sagging mattress and rough sheets faded into insignificance as her body screamed for respite, a need so urgent it drowned out any discomfort.

Yet, as she teetered on the edge of sleep's tenuous embrace, the relentless shadows of her past tightened their grip. Like relentless phantoms, the memories she had fiercely fought to bury clawed their way to the surface, turning her refuge into a battleground.

In the profound silence of the night, the horrors she had endured reawakened as vivid nightmares, pulling her back through the visceral anguish and dread she believed she had escaped.

Her mother and father—gone, claimed by the explosion that obliterated their London home. She heard her mother cry, 'Get Rose,' a desperate command piercing through the chaos. The acrid smell of gas hung in the air. They dragged her through what was once the front wall. Then came the explosion. Every pounding heartbeat, every ragged breath in that darkened room mirrored the monumental psychological odyssey that had led her to this precarious moment of solitude. Her mother and father perished in the wreckage of their home, victims of that fateful bomb.

The morning light crept through the window too soon, casting a pale glow that did nothing to soothe her weary soul. The war, which should never have been, relentlessly wore down her mind, a tempest-ridden battlefield.

For three long years, she had devoted herself to stitching together shattered bodies and offering a fragment of hope to wounded souls clinging desperately to the promise of a reunion with their loved ones.

Today, she would once again step into the storm. Why? Because she couldn't stand the thought of them suffering alone, adrift in their sea of pain. She refused to become a reflection of the cruelty that humanity had unleashed upon itself. Where had the kindness of humankind vanished?

Before facing the growing list of work tasks, she reached out to her lifeline, Aunt Rosemary, whose wisdom and love had always been a steady anchor in her life.

The old rotary phone on the wall was a relic of times past, yet it was her lifeline to cherished voices. She gingerly lifted the receiver and dialled, each click of the numbers blending with the gentle hum of dawn outside.

The familiar ringtone echoed in her ear, a symphony of anticipation and nervousness, until a warm but slightly crackly voice finally emerged, filling the space with comforting familiarity.

'Hello, Rosemary Ashford.'

'Aunt Rosemary, it's me, Rose.'

'Rose, how nice to hear from you.' Her cheerful voice brightened the day. 'How are you faring? I hear they have been bombing London again.'

'Yes, it does not seem to stop. We scuttle like crabs into the bunkers every time the siren sounds.'

Her Aunt's voice, filled with concern, said, 'You keep yourself safe.'

'I will. I was calling to find out if you knew any Andersons in Windermere. Her Aunt was silent, so an Australian soldier had burns. He's in a bad way and keeps murmuring, 'Windermere.''

Static hissed in her ear; she heard her Aunt catch her breath. Then she whispered. 'Yes... Yes, I knew the Andersons. Hugh went to Australia.'

'Are you okay?' Rose asked, concerned. 'Your voice sounds different.' She knew she was upset, but why?

'Just the line,' her Aunt's voice came clear. 'He went to Western Australia.'

'Thanks, that's great. If the patient survives, I will find out. He said something about my Windermere not being the same as his.' Another nurse was waiting for her to finish. 'I must go. Jenny wants to use the phone. Bye, I will keep in touch.'

'Please do. I want to know if he is Hugh's son.' Aunt Rosemary replaced the handset.

Aunt Rosemary stood, the smell of tea lingering in the air. Soft golden light bathed the room, filtering through the lace curtains and casting delicate shadows on the patterned wallpaper.

Hughes' son injured and in London—a sombre expression crept across her face as she delved into her memories. Hugh couldn't lose his only remaining son, especially after the heartbreak he'd already endured.

A lone, glistening tear traced its way down Aunt Rosemary's cheek, mingling warmth with the coolness of her skin. She shivered slightly at the thought that it could have been her child if things had been different, but that was the past.

She stood determined to shake off the memories. They were only ghosts of the past. A smile gradually lit her face as she moved to the sink, ready to tackle the dishes. She knew the past had to be kept in its place, or it would overshadow the present. She reminded herself to savour today, not to let yesterday's pain cloud it.

As Rose surveyed the ward, she looked at the soldier from the night before, a figure suspended on the delicate thread between life and death. Memories washed over her of their intertwined past and the grit he embodied. Was this the same man who had braved tempests of hardship, driven by a steadfast love for Windamere, cradled in a tranquil that beckoned him home?

Did the prospect of reuniting with beloved faces stir his spirit, or was Windamere's silent call summoning him towards a long-sought peace? She had to know. It was the same man who had braved tempests of hardship, driven by a steadfast love for Windamere and cradled in a tranquillity that beckoned him home.

As she approached the bed, his dark eyes tracked her every movement, remarkably keen and vibrant with life. It was a testament of the tenacity that had carried him through a lifetime of hardship in the Outback, where survival was not a given but a hard-won battle.

'So, you survived the night?' She asked, her voice tinged with relief and the weary resignation from years of witnessing the fragility of life.

He grimaced, a shadow of dread flitting across his rugged face, etched with lines that spoke of countless brushes with death. 'Ah, the English Rose from last night. Didn't think I'd make it, did you?' His Australian drawl was low and musical, like the distant hum of the bush at twilight.

He remembered her, yet he had been semi-conscious. Rose covered her surprise, recalling the way his fevered skin had felt beneath her fingers, and leaned down, her hands now tenderly examining his bandages.

'I've lost so many patients that I've learned not to get my hopes up,' she confessed, thinking of the small graves scattered across the windswept cemetery.

'I will survive.' His voice held a fierce resolve forged in the unforgiving heat and isolation of a lifetime in a far-off land. 'I want to see this 'Windermere' you come from. If fate is kind, perhaps I will show you mine.' He gazed at her with a look that spoke of distant dreams and untamed lands, a promise of adventures neither had imagined.

In his eyes, she saw a fiery determination that defied the grim statistics she had often faced in her career. Memories of past failures flickered through her mind, each a blow to her hope. Yet, there was something uniquely determined about him, and for a fleeting moment, the fragile light within her flickered but did not extinguish. 'I will hold you to that,' she said, clinging to the slim hope that this time might be different.

He watched her retreat, the rhythm of her footsteps a welcome distraction from the relentless pounding in his back. She moved with unwavering grace, her serene face radiating a fresh innocence that seemed incongruous in this grim setting. Yet, beneath that veil of steadfastness, he sensed her weariness, her quiet capitulation to the burdens of this harsh reality. She was his solitary beacon in this chasm of despair—an angel guiding him through this inferno.

She returned with fresh dressings cradled carefully in her hands, her expression a battle between steely determination and understated worry. 'This will hurt,' she whispered, her voice tinged with earnest gentleness. Her eyes, shadowed with fatigue, flickered momentarily with regret as she continued, 'I will try to be gentle.'

Internally, she chastised herself, her thoughts a tumult of frustration and guilt, knowing that nothing could truly ease the pain except for the morphine that lay in such short supply—a cruel irony, for its long-term consequences were as fearsome as its immediate relief.

'Ready.' His face, tense with resolve, portrayed an unwavering determination to seize victory.

Rose was grateful when the pain claimed him, and unconsciousness had once again claimed him; she gently peeled back the bandage, revealing the raw, angry red burns beneath.

Her heart pounded as she meticulously examined the wounds, her breath hitching each time she detected an unfamiliar spot. Relief flooded through her when a thorough search found no signs of infection. She exhaled a shaky sigh, her shoulders loosening slightly from the weight of her fear. Determined, she carefully changed the dressings, each action a silent plea for healing. The antibiotics offered a glimmer of hope, standing as guardians against the looming threat of infection.

Despite all her efforts, an uneasy dread lingered; only time would unveil the actual outcome. Another shift was over, and again, she found herself lost in thoughts of Windamere—a name wrapped in mystery and allure. Windermere is where she grew up, and she has memories of her father and mother. It was the sanctuary where her dear Aunt had nurtured her through the formative years of her life, a nurturing presence now aged and frail whom she missed deeply.

The beauty of Windermere held a special place in her heart, serving as a sanctuary away from the chaos of the war. The serenity of its shores and the tranquillity of its waters gave her a sense of peace and solace amidst the turmoil of the time. It was where she could escape the harsh realities of the conflict and find a temporary respite from the upheaval that had disrupted her life. Windermere's pristine beauty and timeless charm symbolised hope and a connection to happier memories, making it a place of immense importance to her during such trying times.

She cursed the war for cruelly separating them, for this conflict had uprooted so many lives, thrown the world into chaos, and kept her from the comforts of her past. The war had been a series of battles and a relentless force that altered destinies and scattered families. Its repercussions echoed through every facet of her existence, imbuing even her cherished memories with a shade of sorrow. Nevertheless, Windamere remained a constant in her childhood dreams and recollections, even amid the turmoil.

Yet, she couldn't help but ponder his Windermere. What kind of landscape shaped his memories? What stories from his past and his family's history made them name their estate that? The thought intrigued her, binding her nostalgia with a broader sense of shared human experience amidst the relentless backdrop of war.

The ring stops with a resonant click. 'Aunt Rosemary, it's Rose.' She tries to infuse her voice with a touch of cheerfulness.

'Good morning, dear. You don't sound as bright today,' Aunt Rosemary's voice ripples with concern. 'Just a little down,' Rose murmurs, knowing that disguising her true feelings from her perceptive Aunt is futile.

'How is Rory doing?' Aunt Rosemary inquires, her voice tinged with worry.

'He's doing better than expected; he's a fighter,' Rose replies, suppressing a sigh.

'I thought he would be,' Aunt Rosemary responded, the relief palpable in her words; she knew he had the Hughes' resolve.

'Better go. Catch you tomorrow.'

'Goodbye, love,' Aunt Rosemary's voice wavered as it faded down the line.

Rosemary moved to the window, her gaze drifting over the garden below. How was this possible? A thread linking her to Hugh — as if a fractured bond from the past was now stretching forward, seeking to reunite their lives once more.

## CHAPTER 2 - RECOVERY WARD

### Historical Notes

A casualty ward typically featured rows of simple metal-framed beds, each with minimal personal storage, separated by curtains for privacy. The atmosphere was functional but compassionate, with medical staff providing care for war-related injuries such as fractures, burns, and shrapnel wounds.

Rose had been observing Rory's recovery closely and noted daily improvement. His lopsided grin, a heartwarming sight, greeted her warmly each morning, sealing a silent bond between them.

'Good morning, Rose. Still hanging in there with me?' Rory greeted. His voice was a deep, soothing melody that resonated with a comforting warmth she had grown to cherish. His eyes crinkled at the corners as he spoke, reflecting his genuine affection for her.

With a radiant smile, she breathed a bright 'Good morning,' her voice bubbling with cheerful anticipation.

She moved with practised grace, placing fresh dressings on her fingers, and worked gently, ready to change them as part of her comforting routine. Her every movement spoke of her dedication and the quiet strength beneath.

'Is that all I get? Just good morning?' he teased gently, his voice a soothing murmur, eyes dancing with a mischievous sparkle that caught the morning light. 'Perhaps some conversation. I want to know more about your Windamere.'

She smiled, her lips curving into a playful mimicry of his Australian accent. 'My Wind-er- mere.'

Rory's rich, endearing laughter echoed through the sterile hospital ward, infusing it with warmth. 'You mean 'Wind-a-mere'!'

Their banter, a cherished ritual, transcended mere accents. It was a tapestry of shared moments interwoven . An unspoken affection—a testament to the deep connection that had blossomed between them.

'No, it is Windermere,' she insisted, her eyes twinkling with determination.

'Not my 'Windamere,'' he countered with a playful edge in his voice.

'What is your 'Windamere' like?' she asked, emphasising his pronunciation.

Rory's eyes glazed over, lost in the memory of home. 'It's hot, with plains that stretch endlessly, eucalyptus trees rising from the dust, and a farmhouse standing tall like a sentinel in that vast native land.' His voice softened, carrying the warmth of his homeland.

'Not mine,' Rose countered, her words painting a vivid picture. 'Vast lakes, rolling hills, green valleys, ancient forests, and the quaint village where I grew up.'

She ticked them off on her fingers like a meticulous teacher.

'Different,' Rory quipped, a grin spreading across his face.

'Nurse    Ashford, have      you finished?' Matron's authoritative voice interrupted the moment.

'Oops,' Rose murmured before responding, 'Just about.'

His grin widened, eyes gleaming with understanding. 'These Windameres are worlds apart.'

'Windermere,' she corrected him gently, a smile playing on her lips.

He shifted his gaze to the side, his expression a mix of exasperation and amusement. 'The English,' he muttered with a wry smile, 'they always believe they're infallible.'

In just a week, he had improved enough to be transferred to the rehab ward. On the ground floor, a sense of hope pervaded the atmosphere. The ward had large, arched windows that bathed it in natural light and offered a serene view of the sprawling area. These gardens, meticulously manicured with winding paths and blooming flowers, provided a therapeutic escape for the patients, and the staff routinely encouraged exercise, which was crucial for recovery.

Within the confines of the ward, it was as if a tapestry of human endurance unfurled before one's eyes. Each bed held a story of suffering and survival, where the weary and wounded began their arduous journey toward recovery.

The walls, painted in soothing shades of blue and green, bore witness to this epic struggle. They displayed vibrant artwork depicting scenes of nature and hope. Patients engaged in animated conversation filled the air with a hum. Their laughter and shared anecdotes spoke of bonds forged in the fires of hardship, a testament to their resilience.

The side door led to the garden, where every flower seemed to mirror the patients' determination to rise from the depths of their suffering. Each step taken along these paths, each story shared beneath the blooming canopies, wove a narrative of physical and emotional healing, transforming the ward into a sanctuary of recovery and renewal.

After one of Rose's first visits, Noel, lying in the bed next to his, watched her walk away with a longing in his eyes. Her presence lingered like a gentle fragrance, almost palpable in its absence.

Observing his friend's sad gaze, Rory couldn't help but issue a playful warning: 'She's already taken.'

Noel's eyebrows shot up in surprise. 'Like that?' he asked, a hint of disbelief. 'Are you sure?'

Rory nodded with unwavering confidence. 'I am one hundred percent sure,' he declared, his voice firm. I am taking her home with me.'

Noel cocked his head, puzzled. 'Head over heels?'

'Yes,' Rory replied, his eyes softening as he spoke. 'Head over heels in love.' His words carried the weight of undeniable truth.

Noel held out his hand, and Rory shook it. 'Don't let her escape, or I will catch her.' Rory laughed. Looking at his friend's plastered leg, he commented, 'I can run faster than you.'

With a smirk, Noel agreed. 'Undeniable.' 'Where are you from?' Rory asked with curiosity

sparking in his eyes.

'Melbourne, Victoria,' Noel responded, a hint of pride in his voice. 'And you?'

Rory smirked, the typical interstate rivalry flashing through his mind. 'Well, I won't hold it against you,' he quipped. 'Midjal, Western Australia.'

'Where is that?' Noel asked, raising an eyebrow and leaning forward slightly. 'Not the bush?'

'Yes, the bush, wheat belt country,' came the reply, the speaker gesturing with a slight nod as if pointing to a distant horizon.

'Ah, a farmer. I was a photographer.' Noel's tone shifted, a hint of nostalgia colouring his words.

'Where's your camera?' Noel inquired, furrowing his brow in curiosity.

Noel paused, his eyes narrowing thoughtfully. 'Must be in my luggage. I'll have them find it,' he said, his fingers tapping lightly on his chin as if punctuating his resolve.

This simple exchange was where it all began. Despite the well-known rivalry, something about Noel's straightforwardness and Rory's easy-going nature just clicked. They soon discovered shared interests in sports and politics. As common ground unfolded, their budding friendship deepened, defying the often superficial state-based tensions. It was a moment that marked the beginning of a bond neither would have expected.

Once Noel had his camera, he dedicated countless hours to capturing the world around him. With each click of the shutter, he documented not only the tangible elements of their existence but also the intangible essence of their ongoing battle. He carefully recorded every fleeting moment that stirred in the vicinity, weaving a rich tapestry of visual memories that chronicled the trials and tribulations they faced. In this way, Noel became both an observer and a participant, his photographs assembling an intricate narrative of their shared struggles.

Every day, Rose's arrival felt like a sacred ritual, intertwining solace and torment that seeped into the very essence of Rory's existence. Initially, the salve she applied was merely a balm, a fleeting escape from his persistent discomfort. Yet, with passing time, it morphed into something deeper—an intricate tapestry of pain woven with hints of ephemeral joy. Her touch, once clinical, evolved into a gentle caress that ignited a roiling tempest within him.

"Off with your shirt," Rose chirped, her voice light as a breeze, blissfully unaware of the havoc she was unleashing on Rory's fragile soul.

With a heavy sigh, Rory peeled the shirt from his body, meeting her gaze with eyes laden with unspoken words—a silent cry she seemed unable to comprehend. His shoulders slumped, a gesture thick with yearning and frustration, as he sank onto the bed, turning to face the mattress, his heart burdened with turmoil that went unexpressed.

"It's looking good," she commented, a note of satisfaction lacing her voice, oblivious to the storm raging inside him.

Struggled to hold back a wave of confessions, fighting against the constraints of self-restraint. What seemed progress to Rose felt like a torturous exercise in self-control to Rory, one that he was afraid he would ultimately fail.

His only comment was a 'Hmm.' Looking sideways, Noel caught his eye. The raised eyebrows and cheeky grin confirmed Rory's growing suspicion: Noel had uncovered his secret.

'That's it,' Rose declared, satisfied, and wiped her hands on a towel. Rory turned his gaze toward her, noting the satisfaction lighting up her face.

She did not know that her touch conveyed more than simple care; it was a soothing balm to his restless spirit.

'What are you grinning about?' Rose asked, her curiosity piqued.

'I would say you did a superb job,' Noel butted in.

Rory bristled silently, wishing he could erase that cocky grin from Noel's face. Being the subject of amusement was not his forte; he preferred to keep his vulnerabilities well-guarded.

'Thank you, Noel,' Rose replied, accepting the remark as a genuine compliment. Rory silently appreciated her, grateful for her unaware comfort amidst the subtle tension within him.

The following day, she arrived with a sense of purpose, ready to shoulder her responsibilities. However, she learned that someone had already completed the task. A wave of confusion washed over her as she stood still, the surrounding nurses exchanging knowing glances that spoke of her unfulfilled duty.

"Rory, what's happening?" she asked, her voice tinged with bewilderment.

Stepping in, Noel took charge, his tone steady. "Old Fran made her rounds early today." He left out the background of his own decision, a detail that hung in the thick air between them. Old Fran was a formidable presence, her physique resembling a solid brick fortress, strong enough to withstand any storm. While Noel spared no words on the lines etched across her face, a testament to her years, everyone recognised the warmth of her heart, shining like pure gold beneath the surface.

It hadn't escaped Rory's notice that he'd picked her, joking about his back pain while desperate for someone who could balance toughness with care — much to the amusement of the entire ward.

"How about a stroll in the garden?" Rory proposed, eager to shed the skin of his unofficial role as the ward's jester, even if just for a moment.

As he guided Rose through the ward, the weight of unspoken camaraderie hung in the air, punctuated by the unvoiced chorus of laughter from the men.

On their daily walk in the garden, Rory drew her closer with his arm around her back. 'They are discharging me back to the barracks next week,' Rory announced.

Rose felt a sharp pang of sadness coursing through her. Rory had become the unexpected light in her otherwise predictable and grey existence, his humour and warmth etching unforgettable moments into her heart. Now, as his days in the hospital waned to a close, the looming reality of his departure filled her with a profound reluctance to let him go.

'You're not going back to the war, are you?' she asked, her voice trembling. Visions of Rory's lifeless body sprawled on a distant, violent battlefield seized her mind, and an icy wave of horror gripped her heart.

'Not quite,' Rory responded, his grin faltering as a chilling wind tousled his hair. *Home,* he thought, but what did that even mean? The words echoed in his mind, each a reminder of the emptiness that had settled in his heart.

He felt the burden of his years pressing down on him, a relentless tide of bitter wisdom and the crushing weight of war's weariness. He glanced at the world around him, its colours muted, stripped of vibrancy by the memories of fallen comrades and the haunting spectre of unending conflict.

'Is there a place for me in this chaos?' he wondered, the question an ache deep within his soul. Rory's thoughts spiralled into the labyrinth of his past, vivid flashes of those he had lost flickering before his eyes. Faces of forever young comrades haunted his dreams and waking moments alike. Each smile lost, each voice silenced, tugged at the frayed edges of his sanity. He could almost feel the weight of their sacrifice on his shoulders, a mantle he found too heavy to bear.

His heart clenched with fear at the thought of returning to the battlefield. The very idea of donning his uniform once more, of stepping into the war, filled him with dread. What if he wasn't strong enough? What if he couldn't protect those around him? The self-doubt gnawed at him, festering into a wound that refused to heal.

Did he even deserve Rose's affection, to be loved by someone untouched by the horrors he had seen? The hospital's sterile walls offered a temporary sanctuary, a refuge where he could hide from the chaos of war. But leaving meant facing his demons, confronting the phantoms that trailed his every step.

The thought of leaving Rose behind shackled him to his fears. Rory hesitated, the spectre of his past gripping his soul with icy fingers as shadows of the battlefield loomed ever more prominently in his mind. He wrestled with the tempest brewing inside him.

How could he ever repay a beautiful woman to whom he owed his very life? Though a grin flickered across his face, it couldn't mask the sorrow that shadowed his eyes as memories cast a darkness over his heart.

'I am going home to Windamere?' she asked, a smile playing on her lips despite the flutter of excitement and anxiety. 'I'm taking a week off to visit my Windermere.'

'I suspect they are quite different,' he replied, as her voice pulled him back to the present. His uneven grin failed to hide the fear in his gaze.

'Why don't you come with me?' she blurted out, startling herself. Where had that come from?

They had struggled for his survival, each minute a gruelling test of fortitude and faith. Perhaps the triumph they shared encouraged her, the feeling that they had already conquered so much together. Did he sense the same pull, the complex and suffocating tangle of emotions that now enveloped her in a storm of inner conflict?

Rory pondered this momentarily, a familiar pause descending upon her like the weight of a thousand unspoken words. Each decision and every change demanded thorough scrutiny. He was a man of caution, a quality perhaps honed during the turbulent war years that had scarred their lives and reshaped their very beings. The brutal lessons of the battlefield had deepened his vigilance, moulding him into someone who measured every step with almost eerie precision.

'Yes, I would like that,' he replied softly. His grin returned, though it was now merely a ghost of the broad, joyful smile that used to light up his face, hinting at the shadows of happier times long past.

Later, back in the ward, Noel's eyes sparkled with mischief as he challenged him. 'Well, did you ask her?' he demanded, anticipation curling in the air.

The entire ward seemed to lean in, waiting on tenterhooks for his reply.

A lump formed in his throat as he uttered a reluctant 'No.'

Disappointment rippled through the room, and a chorus of boos swallowed his voice, sealing his shame. 'Coward,' someone hissed from the corners, 'what's wrong with you?'

Before the gloom fully descended upon him, he quickly added, 'But she invited me to go to Windermere, her home.' He felt a flicker of hope ignite, offering him some solace against the tide of disapproval.

'That's better,' Noel said, his voice taking on a teasing edge. 'Even a slow country boy like you should be able to achieve that.' Despite Noel's ribbing, he felt a sense of warmth and camaraderie. The words stung, but beneath the teasing, he sensed a small amount of encouragement, and that was enough.

It was time for Rory to leave, time for goodbyes. 'I am going to miss you guys,' he announced, a profound sadness settling in the room like a heavy fog.

He shook Noel's hand, their grips lingering for a moment. 'Victoria may be the end of the earth,' he teased with a bittersweet smile, 'but keep in touch.' Noel's eyes widened with a mix of sorrow and surprise. 'Yes, I will do that. I will write,' he said. His voice was trembling slightly. Then, attempting to lighten the mood, he added, 'You can write, can't you?'

Rory chuckled softly, tousling his hair in a self-conscious gesture. 'Sure can. Even country boys get an education, an Aussie.'

He turned away, addressing the entire ward to sound cheerful.

'Good luck, guys.' The room echoed with heartfelt wishes and tearful goodbyes.

As Rory approached the door, the group broke into an off-key chorus of 'We'll Meet Again,' resonating with hope and desperation, 'I don't know where, I don't know when. We'll meet again some sunny day.'

As he was about to step out, the cheers intensified into a unified shout, 'For God's sake, ask her.'

## CHAPTER 3 - AUNT ROSEMARY'S COTTAGE

### Historical Notes

A classic Windermere cottage set in a picturesque countryside, 1945. The cottage showcases traditional architectural features typical of the Lake District, including a steeply pitched roof with thatch or slate tiles, small dormer windows, and whitewashed stone walls. The neatly framed windows with flower boxes add charm and warmth to its appearance.

At last, they stepped onto the train platform, where a vibrant whistle sliced through the air, announcing the steam train. A dramatic plume of mist rose, curling around them like a ghostly embrace, as the weariness of their five-hour journey faded into the backdrop.

Rose's eyes twinkled with excitement as she turned to Rory, her voice bright against the backdrop of flitting birds and rustling leaves. 'Isn't it wonderful, Rory? This place feels like a dream.'

Rory's gaze drifted over quaint houses with chimneys releasing warm wisps of smoke, signalling comfort and home. 'It does. They're like scenes from a storybook,' he replied, their charm igniting his senses.

Rose pointed towards the hills, her arm sweeping over the horizon. 'Look at those hills! They stretch out like a green quilt. It's so peaceful compared to London.' She inhaled deeply, savouring the crisp air, a content smile breaking across her face as she relished the calm far removed from the city's relentless pace.

Rory admired Rose's enthusiasm for the simple beauty of Windermere and pulled closer into her orbit of excitement. Rose's gaze shifted to the shimmering lake, her wonder immense. 'Did you know it's England's largest natural lake? Isn't it incredible?' Light danced on her face, illuminating the captivating scene.

'Rose, you're back!' a voice burst forth, electrifying the air.

A smile bloomed on her face, yet worry flickered in her eyes as she replied, 'Windsor!' They embraced the warmth of familiarity like a soft blanket, yet a storm was brewing beneath the surface.

Rory observed an itch of resentment gnawing at his insides as Windsor swaggered in, the embodiment of effortless aristocracy, clad in his rustic finery.

Rose made the obligatory introductions. 'This is Rory Anderson, Windsor Hubert.' The air grew thick with unspoken tension as Windsor extended his hand, a gesture of camaraderie that made Rory instinctively recoil.

Hesitation hung between them like a taut wire before Rory clenched Windsor's hand, scepticism rippling through the touch.

'Windsor,' he replied sharply, the name slicing through the air, heavy with implications.

'An Australian,' Windsor remarked, his voice dripping with polished English precision.

'Yes,' Rory shot back, his tone revealing an unseen edge. There was no need for niceties; each word felt like a duel, a clash of worlds colliding.

'And a soldier,' Windsor continued, his gaze lingering on the uniform that spoke volumes in silence.

Rory held his tongue, allowing the weight of his unspoken truth to hang in the air. He wanted to bark back, 'We fought for England.'

Rose mentioned that Rory had served in Normandy, intending to dissolve the tension between the two men.

'You did not fight?' Rory's piercing gaze locked onto Windsor, a tempest of intensity in his eyes.

Windsor felt a wave of discomfort wash over him. The question landed heavily, resonating with an unsettling truth. No, he had not gone to war; his mother had forbidden it, declaring him the heir. How often had he endured the weight of judgment for his mother's unwavering refusal? Each word felt like a dagger, igniting the turmoil within him as he grappled with the haunting shadows.

'No, I had to manage the estate; my parents are aging,' Windsor replied, but the explanation felt flimsy in Rory's judgment. Memories of his mother's solitary toil on their farm gnawed at his conscience.

'Really,' Rory said, his gaze drifting into recollections of shared hardships and unrelenting responsibilities.

'Let's go. Aunt Rosemary is waiting,' Rose interjected, sensing their shifting animosity. 'Are you here only for the weekend?' Windsor's inquiry dripped with ulterior motives, curiosity intertwined with something more profound.

'A week, then back to work,' Rose replied, her hesitance echoing the uncertainty that cloaked the moment.

Windsor's eyes bore into hers with an earnestness that felt urgent. 'Join us for dinner on Sunday,' he insisted, warmth mingling with an underlying tone of pressure. His invitation extended to Rory as if he were an afterthought: 'All of you, even Aunt Rosemary.'

'Will your mother approve?' Rose asked, a flicker of doubt tainting her voice.

'No worries,' Windsor waved off her concern.

Yet the dismissive gesture did little to ease the tension that rippled through Rory. Although he doubted the company would impress his mother.

'Thank you, we would love to come.' She responded, a smile attempting to mask her lingering hesitation. Windsor's sudden interest unsettled her—was it sincere affection or veiled competition? She felt a dissonance between his surface charm and the storm brewing in Rory's heart, a deep understanding of love that Windsor seemed to lack.

Beside her, Rory's displeasure simmered like lava beneath a fragile crust. The invitation festered within him, an unwelcome intrusion.

'I'll send a car for you at six,' Windsor announced, turning to descend the hill, leaving a wake of unresolved feelings behind.

Rory watched him leave—resentment across his features. The bitterness of Windsor's cavalier mention of servants stings like a fresh wound. The insidious threads of superiority wove themselves through their exchanges, each word a reminder of the societal gulf that yawned before him.

While Rory had always found pride in his humble beginnings, the yawning chasm between their lives stung sharply. His childhood home was one of toil — a realm where every minor triumph demanded grit and blood, while Windsor glided through life on paths of gold, his every whim effortlessly satisfied.

Beneath the surface, Rory wrestled with feelings. Inadequacy haunted by the notion that, no matter his efforts, the shadows cast by men like Windsor would forever loom ominously over his ambitions. The stark divide they represented tormented him, barriers he feared he would never indeed evade — not in England, at least. Thank the stars for Australia. But what of Rose? He hoped that bringing her to a land of meritocracy would fulfil their dreams, yet dread lingered.

These thoughts enveloped him as they walked along the road toward Rose's Aunt's home, the unsteady pulse of their burgeoning connection weaving between them like a delicate thread, poised to either strengthen or fray at any moment.

'What do you think?' Rose inquired, her voice tinged with eager curiosity. As they turned the corner and Aunt Rosemary's home came into view, the autumn wind whispered through the trees, carrying the scent of fallen leaves and the distant chatter of woodland creatures.

'It's like my Windamere!' Rory laughed when he saw the house at the end of the lane. He grinned widely. Rory studied the roofline; it was his Windamere. There were differences; he had a big porch, and the roof was less steep. He concluded, 'Our Windameres are alike in spirit. Mine is the Australian version. They are similar.'

His excitement surprised Rose. 'What do you mean by similar?' she asked, furrowing her brow in confusion.

'My father built our Windamere and modelled it on your Aunt's house,' Rory explained, his eyes sparkling with nostalgia and pride. His hand reached up to scratch the back of his neck absently, a wistful smile touching his lips. 'Or as close to it as possible, considering the different country and climate.'

As the memory flickered to life, he felt himself swept away, back to Windamere—the sprawling homestead in the heart of Australia's vast plains. There, the golden grass swayed like a sea, and the sky was an endless expanse of deep, inviting blue. How long had it been since he'd stood there, feeling the sun's warmth on his face and the whisper of the breeze enveloping him?

Now, the only anchor he had left was his father — the sole remnant of the family they had once been. His heart ached as he considered the fragile connection, a thin lifeline tethering him to a past brimming with love and warmth. The war had ravaged their world, snatching away his mother, Albert, and Guy, leaving behind an emptiness he struggled to comprehend.

The sounds of their laughter, which used to fill the air with palpable joy, had faded into a haunting silence that would cling to the walls of Windamere like an unwanted guest.

Could this place ever reclaim the essence of home? Would it ever again resonate with the spirit of the love they had shared? The price of the war, so steep and unforgiving, demanded more than he could bear, and in its wake, it offered nothing—only echoes and shadows of what once was.

Rose took a deep breath to calm herself. The air was thick with the scent of freshly cut grass and eucalyptus, a symphony of a distance with the wind-whispered secrets of the ancient oaks.

Silence enveloped them as Rory's gaze lingered on the house, a familiar yet subtle version of his home.

'Father was trying to capture your Aunt's home, but the setting is so different,' he mused inwardly, his eyes reflecting the myriad emotions cascading through him like autumn leaves caught in a gentle breeze.

Rory could see the sun's golden rays shining on the veranda boards, casting shadows that seemed to whisper tales of the past. Windamere was his father's pride, as it stood out amongst smaller homes in Midjal. His father had built it to honour love with perseverance. This home must have meant a great deal to him for him to use it as a model.

'So you have my Windermere.' Rose's eyes sparkled with a mischievous glint as she tried to coax more out of him.

There was a playful energy about her, a cheeky side that Rory found both surprising and endearing, especially considering the hardships she had faced during her nursing experience. The contrast between her light-hearted demeanour and the gravity of her work made her all the more intriguing to him.

'No, mine is Wind-a-mere.' He raised an eyebrow, 'With an a.'

As they approached the end of the lane, the anticipation of home wrapped around them like the sweet scent of autumn leaves.

'So this is where Father's idea came from?' Rory murmured, viewing Aunt Rosemary's house for the first time. It was different but enough alike to be recognisable.

'Aunt Rosemary's house?' Rose asked, puzzled.

'Windamere is bigger and adapted to the hotter climate, but you can see the likeness in the roofline.'His grin widened.

The door opened, and Aunt Rosemary stepped out, opening her arms to Rose. Their affection was obvious, but not so their appearance. Aunt Rosemary was robust and shorter, her face open and happy. Rose was younger, taller, and more beautiful, her dark hair gleaming in the sunlight.

Remembering Rory's presence, Rose stepped back. 'This is Rory,' she introduced him.

Aunt Rosemary caught sight of Rory. He resembled Hugh, but his mischievous grin, hinting at his father's spirited nature, was absent. The war still weighed on him.

Memories of her youth surged as she recalled the laughter that once filled her childhood home. She turned to face Rory, her heartwarming emotions long forgotten.

'You must be Hugh's son!' she said, her voice rich with excitement and nostalgia. Her eyes were sparkling, with untold stories. A hug was what her smile felt like, it bridged past and future. Her greeting was heartfelt: 'Welcome to our family, welcome home.'

'Thank you,' he replied, stepping to shake her hand, only to find himself in her embrace.

Once free, he grinned widely. 'You must be Aunt Rosemary!' he laughed. 'From the Ashford side, I assume?' His eyes gleamed with curiosity.

'Indeed, an Ashford,' she replied, her voice brightened by merriment. 'The last of the Windermere Ashfords,' she added softly, nostalgia washing over her. 'And you are Hugh's son, just like him.'

Gathering herself, she ushered them through the door into the cozy cottage.

'You show him to the guest room while I set up tea,' Aunt Rosemary commanded.

Rory trailed behind Rose down the corridor, her cheerful footsteps echoing softly against the walls. As they reached the last room, a warm and inviting glow enveloped him, starkly contrasting the shadowy corners of his home, where the tight grip of financial worry stifled laughter and warmth. A longing surged within him, a bittersweet reminder of the comforts that felt perpetually out of reach, making the cozy space seem almost foreign in abundance.

'I'll unpack for a bit,' she offered, her fingers brushing against the worn fabric of the suitcase as if it held more than just clothes; it was a vessel of memories waiting to be released. 'Go on,' she encouraged, her tone laced with warmth and a touch of mischief. 'Aunt Rosemary's going to want to hear about your dad.' Her eyes sparkled with intrigue, a hint of unspoken secrets lingering in the air, weaving an invisible thread connecting the past.

Rory corrected her with a cheeky grin. 'Windamere,' he emphasised before departing.

'Not 'a' but 'er," Rose called after him.

Aunt Rosemary guided him to a chair at the table and then went to the old stove, where warm scones were ready.

Rory couldn't help but compare it to his home, 'Windamere.' Her place felt cozy and warm, while his 'Windamere' felt empty and unfinished. Although the houses looked similar outside, her Windamere felt alive and welcoming, a natural family haven.

'Rose mentioned the 'Windamere,' an intriguing Australian variation of the word,' Aunt Rose mentioned, her voice lingering softly in the air.

'Did she?' Rory asked with interest.

Aunt Rosemary gracefully placed a large, ornate teapot on the table, its surface reflecting the soft afternoon light. Alongside it, a platter of freshly baked scones was set with care, emitting a warm, buttery aroma. Cups and saucers rattled as she arranged them delicately, and the fine china plates gleamed subtly.

'Calcutta' is where the story starts. ' A hotel built by a family from Windamere, the hotel could not use Windamere for legal reasons, so they abbreviated it to Windamara. So your Windamere came from here, but your father wanted no confusion, so he named it Windamere.'

They laughed together.

Her warm and nostalgic eyes met Rory's. 'I knew your father. We were best friends many moons ago,' she added, a tender smile touching her lips as memories seemed to flicker like golden leaves in the autumn of her mind.

'You knew Dad?' Rory's curiosity was piqued, and the pieces clicked together.

'Yes, I knew him well. He dreamed big, always talking about turning his barren land into a thriving farm. And he did it,' she reflected with admiration.

'He certainly poured everything he had into building our home. Every brick and beam carries a piece of his dedication,' Rory added. He left out that despite his tireless efforts, his father never succeeded as a farmer. The crops often failed, the livestock dwindled, and financial struggles were a constant shadow. Yet, none of that dimmed the significance of the house he had built for them.

Aunt Rosemary remembered when Hugh Anderson asked her father for permission to marry her. Her father said no. 'A miner's life is only poverty and despair. I want more for Rosemary.' These words hurt them both in different ways. Hugh was brave and determined, asking her to move to Australia. But she couldn't be as bold as he was, and she cried as she said goodbye. Was there regret? Torn between sorrow and comfort, she chose the latter.

The memory hurt her with what-ifs and missed chances. But the life she chose brought her peace with its familiarity and stability. She often wondered how things might have been if she had gone with Hugh.

'He has a life that would have always escaped him here,' Rosemary whispered, feeling the heavy weight of her father's shadow. Her fingers traced the worn edges of an old photograph, imagining dreams that had turned cold. Tears welled as she remembered her father, blind to Hugh's true self beneath the miner's grime. That fleeting clarity vanished like mist. Her heart ached, each beat a testament to the courage required now. Love felt like a fleeting memory, a fragile dream dissolved.

'Yes, he has achieved much, especially as a miner,' Rory added.

'Enough memories,' she commented, her voice tinged with a hint of finality. 'Tomorrow, Rose will show you our Windermere.' A flush of colour bloomed in her cheeks, like the first blush of dawn over the tranquil lake beyond the rolling hills, and a broad smile spread across her face. She buried the past, now just memories.

Rory continued. 'Do I have any relatives?' he asked, his eyes searching for a way out of the oppressive tension that hung like a dense fog.

'No, they are all gone,' Rosemary replied, her voice tinged with a bittersweet sadness. As she spoke, memories of her father's sombre words replayed, each syllable painting a stark picture of their lives.

Poverty, he had often remarked, was an unyielding affliction that gnawed at both the body and soul, with death as the sole deliverance. This bleak destiny felt inevitable for a miner trapped in his worn-out boots, the relentless wind whistling mournfully through the cracks of his decrepit shack in Windermere. Dust clung to his skin, mingling with sweat, as he toiled in the suffocating darkness of the mines, his breath echoing against the cold, unforgiving walls.

Despite the heavy pall of their shared history, Rosemary was resolute in her desire to give Rory some measure of belonging. 'But we will show you where your father lived and introduce you to the people who knew him.'

She felt the inadequacy of her offering, like trying to fill a hollow void with small tokens of the past, but it was the best she could offer.

Thankfully, Hugh had escaped the grim destiny that claimed many of his kin—a fate carved in the mines of a distant land across the oceans, where shadows of the future loomed dark and unyielding.

# CHAPTER 4 - WINDERMERE'S SECRET

## Historical Notes

Rory's grandparents' cottage stood weathered and weary, its walls of rough-hewn local stone whispering tales of countless seasons. The slate tiles on the roof, once a deep charcoal, now bore cracks and patches of moss, shifting under the weight of time and relentless rain. A faint scent of damp earth and aged timber filled the air, mingling with the soft rustle of wind through nearby trees. Inside and out, the cottage Fexuded a quiet melancholy, a lingering echo of a world long passed—an era where one's place was at birth. The rigid English social order pressed down like the thick fog that often settled over the landscape—impenetrable and cold. Above, the aristocracy revelled in their inherited grandeur, while below, the working class toiled in dim factories and cramped quarters, their weary bodies and spirits worn thin by meagre wages and harsh conditions. The cottage, abandoned and silent, stood as a poignant relic of this stark divide, a testament to lives shaped and shadowed by birthright and struggle.

Aunt Rosemary, known for her warm demeanour and sharp wit, had gracefully declined the walk around Windermere, attributing it to the frailty of her aging legs. However, the real reason was far more poignant. She saw this as a precious moment for Rory and Rose that she should not intrude upon.

Standing just outside the door, she watched them stroll down the road, a bittersweet smile touching her lips. The panorama of her past unfurled before her — memories of lost opportunities and Rose's dreams never entirely realised.

Her love for Hugh had always been a unique tapestry of shared history and unspoken words. Their connection was strong, yet neither had ever put it into words. As the years passed and life left its marks on Rosemary's face, she reflected more on the potential for love to bloom fully in Rory and Rose's newfound companionship.

She could picture them growing closer through evening strolls in the park, hearty laughs shared over dinner, and whispered conversations by the fire. She hoped that, unlike the wistful dream that had lingered unfulfilled between her and Hugh, this relationship could find its happy ending.

They stood before his grandparents' home, where his father had grown up, with a feeling of overwhelming despair. The despair clung to the crumbling walls while the wind mourned through the broken windows. They were gone, lost, and only surviving in memories. His father had survived, and his decision to make Australia home was wise.

The relentless trials honed his skill set and determination here as well. Day after arduous day, he used those skills to delve into the unforgiving earth of Kalgoorlie, his hands bruised and weary from the countless hours spent chipping away at stubborn rock faces that guided him to hidden veins of gold. Every nugget discovered was a hard-won victory, a testament to his painstakingly acquired expertise and steadfast resilience. In this crucible of sweat and grit, he forged a modest fortune, an indomitable spirit, and deep, hard-earned respect from fellow miners.

Driven to surpass his parents, he succeeded beyond measure, building Windamere as a testament to emulate Aunt Rosemary's home, which must have held special memories. Aunt Rosemary's home was warm and welcoming, safe and gentle, far removed from the house he had. It was everything I had desired.

She embodied a realm of elegance, steadiness, and soft nobility in his eyes. Her home brimmed with radiant light and joyous laughter, radiating a profound sense of comfort and belonging that his own house sorely missed.

It was not merely wealth that drove his father, but the pursuit of an ideal, the longing to recreate the tender memories of summers spent in Aunt Rosemary's gardens, where roses and camaraderie thrived equally.

A profound sorrow settled within Rory as he reflected on his father's accomplishments. Vivid memories of his father's ever-present smile, masking the depths of his struggles, played through his mind. He couldn't help but wonder if his father had ever truly grasped the magnitude of what he had achieved. How much deeper would his father's sorrow be now, knowing he returned as the lone surviving son? Albert, who always shared stories of their childhood escapades at Windamere, and Guy, whose laughter could brighten even the darkest days.

He felt the chilling slick of sweat bead on his forehead; each drop was a harbinger of the war memories surging forth—the gut-wrenching terror, the visceral sight of endless carnage with blood-soaked fields and haunting cries. He stood there, pallor seizing his face as his eyes glazed over, lost in the riptide of recollection.

'Hugh,' Rose called, her voice tinged with worry, as she gently shook his arm. 'Hugh,' she repeated, her grip tightening and her shaking more insistent. She had witnessed this agonising scene countless times, the grip of war dragging him back into its darkness.

'Sorry,' he murmured, placing his trembling hand over hers.

'That will never happen,' he uttered with a note of grim finality.

The aftermath of his experiences left him fragile and profoundly nostalgic, a deep ache for home gnawing at his core. An insistent and overpowering desire surged within him — to craft a family, to breathe laughter and joy into the halls of Windamere. This yearning pulsed through him, a sincere wish to drown out the lingering whispers of sorrow with a radiant harmony of laughter and vitality to usher in a new dawn of life.

'I think it is time for a break,' she added with a spring in her step.' A drink at Riggs.'

They walked in silence, the crisp air filling their lungs while their eyes lingered on the quaint charm of the village. The muted sounds of birdsong and distant chatter provided a soothing backdrop as they took a moment to gather their thoughts.

The cobblestone streets, lined with ancient oak trees, seemed to hum with stories from a bygone era. The day before, they had passed the old hotel that stood a short distance from the railway station, but Rose had been eager to see her Aunt.

Opened initially as a coach house, it once catered to weary travellers using the newly completed railway from Oxenholme to Windermere. Now, the hotel has become a beloved landmark among the locals. Its peaks, sharply outlined against the sky,

Accentuated the attic windows and roofline, stood proudly against the edge of the roadway, adding a sense of stability to the village.

Flowering vines clung lovingly to its walls, and the garden, bursting with colour, seemed like a scene from a painter's canvas. Inside, the warm glow of lanterns allows guests to pause and enjoy the timeless elegance preserved over the years.

The bar's warm glow beckoned them inside.

'Rose, back from London,' the barman greeted with a broad smile.

'Just for a few days. Then back to the hospital,' Rose replied, her eyes reflecting a tired resolve.

'So many lost,' the barman sighed, focusing on Rory. Have you seen action?'

'Yes,' Rory confirmed, extending his hand.' 'Jack,' the barman responded, shaking Rory's hand heartily.

'Australian, eh? I don't see many of you around here. Take a seat,' he gestured towards a table by the window overlooking the bustling street. 'Hugh went to Australia. Haven't heard from him in years,' he added, nostalgia colouring his voice.

'My father,' Rory stated.

'Your father,' Jack's face lit up with recognition. 'Did he do well?'

'Found success in the gold mines,' Rory shared.

'He was a good miner,' Jack reminisced, hinting at wistfulness in his tone. 'Pity Rosemary's father didn't let them marry. He had ambitions for her that she did not share.' Snapping back to the present, he indicated the same table by the window. 'Only a half pint, I'm afraid. Ration's.'

They sat at the table, their minds turning over his words. 'Your father and Aunt Rosemary,' he had said. Rose seemed mesmerised by this revelation.

Rory murmured a thoughtful 'hmm' as he wrestled with the revelation's implications. His mind wandered to his mother.

Had she been aware of this all along? How did she fit into this complex tapestry of connections? Windamere was the culmination of his father's dreams, a lifelong project into which he had poured his soul.

But what of Rosemary? Was she part of this vision, a partner in the dream, or was Windamere a testament to a different kind of love—an attempt to vindicate himself in the eyes of her father's disapproval?

'She never married,' Rose murmured, her voice tinged with curiosity and sadness. 'Do you think that's why?'

Rory's thoughts churned with the day's revelations. Each discovery pressed upon his mind like a weight, making it difficult to think straight. Today was overwhelming—a treasure trove of histories and secrets unearthed, each raising more questions than answers. He felt a pressing need to.

'Drink up. Time to walk home,' he said, trying to force a reassuring smile. He took a long gulp of his ale, the bitter taste sharp against his tongue. He hoped it would help clear the fog in his head. 'I could use a moment to think,' he added, looking towards Rose, hoping she would understand his need for respite.

'Just one thing on the way,' Rose interjected, putting down her glass as she stood up. 'I want to visit my parents' graves. You can head straight home if you'd prefer.'

'No, I'll come,' Rory replied quickly. He didn't want to miss any opportunities to understand Rose better.

Rose paused at a roadside stall to buy wildflowers as they wandered past the railway station. Rory watched as she handpicked each flower, her face a mixture of sadness and resolve.

'These should be nice,' she whispered, almost as if she were talking to her parents directly.

St. Mary's Church was just a short walk downhill from the railway station, with a panoramic view of the shimmering lake and majestic falls rising. The Gothic Revival architecture of the church boasted pointed arches that seemed to reach towards the sky, intricate stonework that felt cool and rough under the fingertips, and stained glass windows through which sunlight flowed.

As Rory strolled through the serene, contemplative atmosphere of the well-kept graveyard, the earthy scent of damp grass and the distant melody of chirping birds filled the air. He noted the variety of tombstones, tracing his fingers over the names on weathered, ancient stones and admiring the polished new ones that stood resolutely amid beds of fresh flowers.

As they walked, Rory couldn't help but compare this graveyard to the one back in Midjal. 'The graveyard at home... it's so different,' he said, almost to himself. 'Windswept hillside, dry ground, barely any vegetation. The headstones are newer and far from ornate.'

'Over here,' Rose guided him, stopping before a well-kept grave plot. She laid the flowers in a corner, her movements slow and deliberate.

'Your family has been here a long time,' Rory murmured, reading the headstone inscriptions, some dated back two centuries.

'Yes,' Rose replied softly, her voice tinged with pride and sorrow. 'This is our family plot; it's almost full.' She kneeled to touch a newer headstone, marking the resting place of her mother and father.

Rory watched her silently, the stark difference to Midjal weighing heavily on his mind. 'So different from Midjal,' he mused again, this time aloud as if trying to find some understanding in the disparity.

As they departed, Rory's gaze fell upon a row of newly turned graves, their gravestones starkly contrasting with the older ones nearby. The stone was light, almost glowing under the mid-morning sun.

He stepped closer and squinted to read the inscriptions, quickly realising these were the graves of soldiers. The air seemed to grow heavier as a profound sadness wrapped around him, squeezing his heart. His mind drifted to the image of his brother's last rest, buried deep in the soil of Normandy. The thought of his brother without a headstone, so far from the embrace of home, sent a shiver down his spine and caused his throat to tighten. The muffled hum of the world felt distant.

Upon their return, they discovered that Aunt Rosemary was not at home, much to their collective relief. Rory had been hoping to avoid confrontation, but that wasn't in the cards. Rose approached him, carrying some salve. Though Rory resented the necessity, the enslaved person was a constant reminder of Normandy, one that would never let him forget.

He must have dozed off, for the clatter of dishes and the mouthwatering aroma of a hearty meal wafting through the air stirred him awake. The familiar scent signalled Rosemary's return. As he roused himself, the lingering warmth of sleep clung to his skin, and he hurriedly dressed.

His mind raced with anticipation and a hint of unease about the conversation ahead. He then made his way to join her, heart thumping gently.

She turned from the stove, a waft of rich, savoury spices swirling in the air. Her cheeks flushed a rosy hue, and a warm smile spread. The soft sizzle of something delicious frying filled the cozy kitchen.

'Hello, how did the day go?' she asked, her voice blending with the comforting clatter of pots and pans. Rory sat at the table opposite Aunt Rosemary, who held the teapot. 'It was good; we visited my father's home and had a half pint at Riggs.'

Rosemary laughed. 'Rations are part of what we must endure because of the war,' she replied. 'You must have met Jack then.'

'Yes, he mentioned you wanted to marry my father,' Rory said.

Rosemary's face froze momentarily before a sunny smile broke out. 'That's bound to come out — village gossip,' she concluded. 'Yes, I was in love with your father, and we wanted to marry, but my father had other plans. It's funny. I thought last night when you mentioned he is now a farmer. My father only saw him as a miner.'

Rory, sensing her relaxed demeanour, felt his tension dissipate. 'I was worried about asking you; I thought it might bring back poor memories.'

Aunt Rosemary laughed, a sound that carried a mixture of wistfulness and joy. 'No, on the contrary, it brings back good times—the best times,' she said, her eyes lingering in a distant, dreamy gaze. 'Your father was the love of my life, but it was not to be.' She paused, sipping her tea slowly, savouring each memory and her drink's warmth.

Her hand reached for a biscuit, its crunch a momentary distraction in her trance.

'We kept in touch, you know. Even when years had passed, he didn't forget. He asked me to be with him again, but by then, my father had fallen ill,' she explained, her voice softening. 'I stayed and nursed him. It was a difficult time, watching someone you love fade away.' Despite the sorrow laced in her words, there was a poignant acceptance in her demeanour. Rather than harbouring resentment for what life had denied her, she cherished the fleeting moments of happiness she had shared with him. She saw him in a new light, a beacon of cherished memories rather than a source of regret, and carefully tucked away the extraordinary times they had without a trace of bitterness.

'He built Windamere for you,' Rory said softly, his voice tinged with admiration and melancholy.

'Yes, he was proving to my father that he could provide everything,' she replied, her eyes reflecting a blend of gratitude and wistful sorrow. 'Even the chance to become a farmer's wife, which I still find unimaginable.' She giggled, but there was a hint of disbelief in her laughter. 'I never thought he would follow through. He was always a miner at heart..

Rory tilted his head, his thoughts drifting back to memories of his father. 'It was Windamere that he truly loved, not the farming,' he said, his words heavy with understanding. He knew his father's flaws well; the man's stubborn nature clashed with the gentleness required for tending the land. 'Farming was never his passion, but building Windamere, giving you a dream realised, was the love that drove him.'

'How is he now?' Rosemary asked. 'I have not seen four him in years, and in that time, we have endured much heartbreak,' he began, his voice tinged with sorrow. Though hesitant to delve into the painful memories, a part of him wanted Rosemary to understand the depth of their suffering, to feel as though she was a cherished part of their family.

'My two brothers,' he paused as if the weight of his words were too heavy to bear, 'they died in the war.' The silence that followed spoke volumes, encapsulating the immense grief he could not bring himself to explain.

'He must be missing you.' Aunt Rosemary mentioned softly.

'Yes, I want to get home.' Rory's voice carried a calm assurance, but beneath the surface, a storm roiled within him.

The farm was waiting for him, its fertile fields now a symbol of solace and burden.

It wasn't just. The wounds of war had scarred more than just the land—they had left deep furrows in his heart, seeding doubts and fears. Would he be able to rebuild what was lost? Would he recognise the person he had become? A heavy sense of unease emerged as he envisioned the battered economy and the challenges looming ahead. The battles had ended, but the struggle was far from over.

# CHAPTER 5 - SIR Reginald

## Historical Notes

In 1946, aristocratic homes in Windermere still displayed their grandeur but were under strain. Many had been requisitioned during the war for hospitals or evacuees, while others faced financial difficulty and a shortage of domestic staff. Some remained private estates, but many were being converted into schools, hotels, or institutions. They stood as proud symbols of heritage, yet their role was shifting from aristocratic dominance to part of Britain's shared cultural and tourist landscape.

The car arrived promptly at 6 p.m.—a sleek Bentley with a poised chauffeur, immediately stirring a wave of disdain within Rory. Every polished surface and impeccable detail of the vehicle seemed to mock him, amplifying his discomfort.

As he sank into the leather seat, a heavy silence enveloped him. Each breath was fraught with a storm of conflicting feelings as the car journeyed toward the Manor.

When they arrived, a gasp lodged in his throat.

The Manor loomed before him, its magnificent and suffocating grandeur nestled amidst a garden so meticulously trimmed that it felt like a testament to meticulous control over nature's wild beauty. The sight was breathtaking and stifling, a heavyweight settling in his stomach, an ominous premonition of the evening awaiting him.

The butler stepped back as the door opened, revealing Windsor's standing in regal splendour. The hallway stretched before them, its immaculate tiles shimmering like polished gemstones beneath the sparkling chandelier's glow.

Rory yearned to brush aside the extravagant display, yet he found himself ensnared by its allure. It clashed violently with his ideals of equality; here, there was no trace of fairness or justice.

In stark contrast, Aunt Rosemary's cottage floated into his thoughts—an embrace of genuine warmth and intimacy. This opulence felt hollow beside that memory, a vehicle for societal validation rather than a true home. The difference was palpable, igniting the tension within him, a reminder of the chasm.

"Good evening," Windsor beamed at the ladies, gazing at Rose and Aunt Rosemary, bestowing them praises that hung like sweet perfume.

Not a flicker of acknowledgment graced Rory's direction as Windsor added, "Thank you, John. I'll guide them through." He offered his arm to Rose, leaving Rory to accompany Aunt Rosemary in a role that again felt secondary.

A tempest brewed inside Rory; the familiar volatility of comparison ignited his spirit, a sensation of being eclipsed again by Windsor. It wasn't merely the sting of being overlooked—it was Windsor's uncanny ability to render him invisible, a dismissal so artful and casual it burrowed under Rory's skin, igniting flames of frustration that simmered just beneath the surface.

Aunt Rosemary tapped his arm. 'Don't let him get to you,' she murmured. 'That is what he wants.'

'By playing Lord of the Manor?' Rory responded quietly, trying to suppress the biting resentment in his voice, but he could not help but feel the sting of condescension.

'Yes, remember his family has been here for centuries,' she smiled, her eyes compassionate yet knowing the brittle pride Rory carried. 'You will, Sir Reginald, be more palatable,' she predicted.

Rory knew she was trying to reassure him. But the weight of Windsor's shadow, a legacy of dominance, which he was struggling to accept, was present.

In a Midjal where everyone shared the same modest means, he was taught from a young age that every person deserved equal respect and opportunities. His father ingrained this ethos in him; he recounted stories of communal efforts and collective triumphs.

However, it wasn't until he found himself amidst the chaos of the battlefields that he encountered the stark contrasts of the English ruling class. There, the elite's deeply entrenched hierarchies and privileges sharply opposed the egalitarian beliefs that had shaped his upbringing.

Aunt Rosemary possessed a keen intuition for discerning character, and her evaluation rang true.

At first glance, Sir Reginald was not the arrogant aristocrat one might expect. Instead, he presented himself as a dignified elder with meticulously styled grey hair and a pleasant demeanour that put others at ease.

Windsor gave them a perfunctory introduction, handing Rose as if she were one of them. In stark contrast stood his wife, Clarissa, with her coiffed blonde hair perfectly poised and her smile dripping with condescension—an apparent snobbery on display. It became all too clear when Aunt Rosemary, with her characteristic warmth, introduced Rory to the couple, and Clarissa's dismissive remark hung in the air like a cloud.

Aunt Rosemary, never fussed or outdone, addressed Sir Reginald. 'You may remember his father, Hugh. He was a miner who bravely ventured to Australia.' Her pride was apparent, her stance was firm amidst the nobility.

'A miner,' Lady Clarissa sniffed, her disdain unmistakable. 'I doubt we would have had the pleasure of meeting him.'

'I remember him well,' Sir Reginald interjected, his tone warming with genuine admiration. 'He was a remarkable miner known for his skill in uncovering gold veins. I assume his efforts brought him success?' His gaze turned expectantly to Rory.

'Indeed, he struck gold in Kalgoorlie,' Rory replied, a mischievous glint in his eyes. 'With his newfound wealth, he transformed our three- thousand-acre farm.' There was a satisfaction in his voice, a sharp contrast to the modesty of English estates, even as he delivered his subtle jibe.

Her husband promptly disregarded Lady Clarissa's dismissive 'Oh'.

'Good for him. I always enjoy seeing my men prosper,' Sir Reginald commented.

Aunt Rosemary remained silent, memories of the miners' harsh working conditions weighing heavily on her.

'Time for dinner,' Lady Clarissa suggested, her eyes lingering on the butler, signalling him with a pregnant and weary glance.

'Certainly, let's go through. Miss Ashford,' Sir Reginald said, a touch of tenderness in his voice as he held his arm out to Aunt Rosemary. His gesture was more than mere politeness; it spoke of a longing to protect and cherish.

With a burst of adrenaline, Rory turned to Rose, holding out his arms, which she readily accepted.

There was no way Rory was escorting Lady Clarissa. He couldn't help but look triumphant when Windsor had to escort his mother.

The dining table sprawled elegantly, capable of hosting a much larger gathering than the mere six who would occupy it. An exquisite display adorned the tabletop, with softly flickering candles and vases overflowing with fresh flowers, which created an enchanting atmosphere.

Rory approached, intending to claim his spot at the far end, but just as he was about to lower himself onto the chair, Sir Reginald's voice pierced through the ambient chatter.

'Rory, come join me at this end,' he beckoned, gesturing emphatically to a seat at his right. His tone was inviting yet charged with a palpable curiosity. 'I would like to learn about Kalgoorlie and Australia.'

Rory's heart quickened at the unexpected attention, his apprehension melting away under the warmth of Sir Reginald's enthusiasm. A smile broke across his face as he felt welcomed into the inner circle of conversation, the camaraderie between them sparking an instant connection.

'Certainly, Sir, I would like that.' Rory's voice quivered slightly, betraying a mixture of eagerness and trepidation as he took his seat. He cautiously glanced at Rose and Aunt Rosemary on the opposite side of the grand table. He was acutely aware of the moment's weight; Sir Reginald deserved the utmost respect with his distinguished presence, and Rory felt a quiet pressure to uphold that decorum.

The elegant surroundings only heightened the tension. Rory's heart swelled with admiration as the attendants glided in the crisp white uniforms—each movement perfectly choreographed. The matching hats were like crowns atop heads, emphasising the grandeur of the affair.

He couldn't suppress a smile, feeling a surge of joy amidst the opulence. Yet, beneath the surface, he grappled with a whirlwind of emotions—wonder, respect, and a touch of envy—each competing for his attention as he absorbed the lavish scene.

So, this was how the other half lived. It was all very grand but not to Rory's taste. He could not fathom how one could ever relax in this environment. To Rory's astonishment, the evening was a success. Sir Reginald's passion for farming drew him in, and they discussed it. As they exchanged ideas, the conversation meandered through the lush fields of England and the sun-drenched expanses of Australia, uncovering the challenges each faced. With each shared experience, the warmth between them deepened, making the night feel alive with possibility.

They departed with the promise of exploring the sprawling fields of Sir Reginald's farm and the mine that had once echoed with his father's labour. The air was thick with anticipation as memories of toil and resilience flickered like distant lanterns in the recesses of minds.

Rory's gaze shifted inward, drawn toward the passions that once ignited his spirit. He struggled to push the haunting echoes of war into the shadows of his memory.

The following morning, he awoke with the sun barely stretching its golden rays across the room, only to be greeted by the delightful clatter of utensils and the rich aroma of breakfast wafting through the air. Aunt Rosemary was already at the table, her warm smile illuminating the cozy kitchen.

'Good morning, Rory,' she beamed, the cheerful tone mingling with the soft bubbling of water on the stove. You're up early today.

Rory settled into his chair, the wood excellent against his fingertips, and glanced at Aunt, what I expected after meeting Windsor.'

'Indeed, Windsor presents a fascinating contrast,' Aunt Rosemary reflected, her spoon idly stirring the porridge that warmed her hands.

Memories surged within her, vivid images of Windsor basking in the relentless adoration of his mother—a situation that struck her as both endearing and troubling. Lady Clarissa, his mother, saw her son as the epitome of perfection; he could do no wrong in her eyes. 'His mother has sheltered him, often at the cost of his father's role in his life. Although somewhat unremarkable, Sir Reginald embodies what we expect from the upper echelons—fair, affable, and a loyal supporter of the societal hierarchy."

Rory, taking a moment to ponder over his spoonful of porridge, finally interjected, "I think your perception of class distinction is misguided. Surely, everyone is equal.

With a dismissive wave, Aunt Rosemary countered, "That ideal is nothing but a dream. The rigid social structure will always rank men we abide by or by their talents and merits."

"While I can accept merit as a measure, I will not subscribe to the notion of enforced class," Rory pressed, his brow furrowed in thought. "Besides Windsor, he seems intent on courting Rose."

"On the contrary," Aunt Rosemary snapped, irritation colouring her words. "His true aim lies in securing your downfall, dear boy. Rose is nothing more than a pawn in his mother's game. His mother, Clarissa, deems us beneath him, and he dances to her tune."

As Rory absorbed her pointed observations, an unsettling truth crystallised. Aunt Rosemary had indeed touched on something profound—Lady Clarissa's influence loomed large, casting long shadows over lives and dictating social standing within her world.

With a contemplative sigh, Rory finally pushed back from the table, the lingering warmth of the porridge punctuating his senses. The flavours and the conversation swirled within him, igniting a myriad of conflicted thoughts about ambition, love, and the inexorable chains of expectation that bound them all. 'Well, I am off to take up Lord Reginald's farm tour,' he announced, his voice carrying a hint of excitement that danced in the steam rising from the

kitchen.

He gathered his empty bowl and walked to the sink, the early morning light streaming through the window and casting a golden hue over the room. As he rinsed his dish, the fresh scent of the farm wafted through the open door, stirring a longing for the sprawling fields that awaited him.

'Thank you for breakfast. I wish you a good day,' he said, his voice warm yet tinged with a subtle longing. 'And please extend my regards to Rose; I should return by lunchtime.'

'I will,' Aunt Rosemary replied, her voice carrying a depth of affection that seemed to wrap around the words —the moment hung delicately between them, like the last notes of a melody echoing through the stillness of the morning.

'Ah, you're early,' Sir Reginald remarked, a joyous smile illuminating his face. The absence of his usual butler added a moment of intimacy to the encounter.

'I trust it's not too early,' Rory replied, a flicker of concern crossing his features as he registered the aging lines on Sir Reginald's face, reminding him of passaging time.

'Not at all, my boy. Though I may be on the other side of my youth, mornings are charming for me. They have a certain crispness, as if the world is breathing anew.' Rory revelled in the English mornings, where the invigorating chill enveloped him like a brisk hug, each breath sharp and alive with potential. The earthy scent of dew-kissed grass awakened his senses and stirred new dreams as it laced the air.

In stark contrast, the mornings in Australia, though charming, felt parched and predictable. Each dawn was a whisper of familiarity, a mere turning of the pages in a well-loved book, lacking the thrill of rebirth that the English sun ignited.

'Well, time to go,' Sir Reginald remarked, gesturing towards the jeep that awaited their departure.

It lacked the usual pomp of a dedicated chauffeur; instead, two men stood by—one older, weathered by years, and the other younger, whose attentive demeanour bore witness to the respect he held for Reginald, transcending mere social status.

The presence offered a glimpse into the subtle dynamics of admiration and duty simmering beneath the surface, hinting at untold stories and connections forged through shared experiences in a world often dictated by rank.

The contrast between Sir Reginald's English farming and Rory's Australian expanse was strikingly vivid.

Rory envisioned his surroundings—endless fields stretching beneath an expansive sky, the golden hues of wheat swaying in the breeze. Such was the reality of Australian wheat and sheep farming.

The farms sprawled across the land, caused by an unforgiving climate characterised by relentless heat, arid conditions, and scant rainfall. To ensure the survival of the crops and livestock, farmers had to gain vast tracts of land.

Wheat farming was a colossal endeavour, marked by the whir of machinery efficiently sowing and reaping the golden grains. Meanwhile, the sheep roamed freely over the sprawling terrain, the woolly forms dotting the landscape as they grazed on the sparse vegetation. Australia exported its wheat to distant Asian markets because it had firmly rooted its agricultural endeavours in the country. Bales of wool found their way to buyers across the globe.

'Rory, have you thought about the significant changes to our farming practices since the war?' concern threaded through his voice as they ambled through the sun-drenched fields.

'You mean the shrinking plots, Sir?' Rory replied, casting a sorrowful glance at the diminished lands. 'It's clear that farmers are scrambling to make the most of the scarce land we still possess.'

'Indeed, my dear Rory,' Sir Reginald continued, his brow furrowing with worry. 'The government's intervention has been less of a lifeline and more of a burden. Those subsidies and the so-called advanced machinery—it feels like they expect us to pull sustenance from the surrounding air!'

Rory chuckled, though the sound held a bittersweet edge. 'It's certainly become a pressing matter. We've all felt the harsh reality of food insecurity after the war. It's almost miraculous how quickly we've had to change course.'

'Ah, the transition to mixed operations,' Sir Reginald mused, a reflective sigh escaping him. 'Embracing a blend of crops, livestock, and even the rare dairy cow—it feels like a necessary strategy given the shortages that still haunt us.'

'Quite a stark difference, isn't it?' Rory added, his voice tinged with nostalgia. 'Back in Australia, we've stubbornly clung to single-crop cultivation, primarily for export. It makes one truly appreciate the gravity of our current situation.'

'Exactly! We must prioritise feeding our people,' Sir Reginald said, his voice rising with conviction. 'As stewards of the land, we have a deeper responsibility—to nourish our nation before all else.'

'I'd like to introduce you to one of our tenant farmers,' Sir Reginald offered, skillfully maneuvering the jeep towards a nearby field. The air buzzed with the scent of rich soil and sunshine.

'In Australia, farms are colossal enterprises, vast expanses that thrust bounty onto the world stage,' he continued, emphasising the vibrant pulse of agrarian life that filled the atmosphere.

'Absolutely! It's remarkable. You gaze upon England, and it transforms into an entirely different narrative,' Sir Reginald elaborated, his voice rich with the weight of tradition.

'Indeed, you still cling to that historical landowner-tenant system,' Rory noted, the contrast sparking curiosity.

'Precisely! Our farmers toil upon rented patches, each plot a testament to resilience and stewardship,' Sir Reginald affirmed, the landscape around them whispering stories of labour and harvest.

Meeting the farmer was interesting. To Rory, he seemed content with his status as a tenant, as his family had for generations—something forcign to an Australian.

For Rory, the disparity was nothing short of astonishing. The spirit of autonomy flourished.

Driving back from the farm, Sir Reginal felt compelled to explain.

'Rory, let me explain this simply.'

'Where I hail from, the sheer expansiveness of our sprawling paddocks, which seem to reach towards the horizon, will strike you,' Rory replied, his eyes wide with the imagery conjured by his memories. 'We own our land and farm with little government help.' He paused. 'But in England, farms are more minor, yet brimming with diversity—crops, livestock, and dedicated hands working earnestly to extract every yield from every inch of earth.

It's not so much a panorama of open fields as it is a testament to the productivity and dedication required.

Sir Reginald insisted on escorting Rory back to Aunt Rosemary's quaint cottage. A silent understanding passed between them, laden with the weight of new beginnings and unresolved paths.

"I can't thank you enough, Sir, for your time and company," Rory said, his voice tinged with gratitude and lingering uncertainty.

Sir Reginal's grip was firm, a tangible reminder of the bond they had forged in such a brief encounter. "Son, you journeyed from the other side of the world for our cause—a choice I admire deeply," he replied, his tone imbued with sincerity as if he was acknowledging a shared mission that transcended mere duty.

'Thank you,' Rory expressed, feeling the warmth of the commendation washing over him, stirring something deep within—the realisation that someone so esteemed acknowledged his efforts and sacrifices.

"I can't accompany you to the mine where your father worked, but I can arrange for Jake to show you around tomorrow if that suits you," Sir Reginal continued, a hint of kindness lighting his features.

"I would appreciate that, Sir," Rory responded, a flicker of hope igniting within him at the thought of connecting with his father's legacy.

"Tomorrow at seven, Jake will wait for you,' Sir Reginal assured him, his eyes holding a weight of promise as he observed Rory preparing to part ways. "Should you ever find yourself in need, call? I will do everything in my power to assist you."

Rory stood rooted to the spot, eyes fixed on Sir Reginald's carriage as it vanished around the bend. His heart churned with a mixture of unease and unexpected comfort. Though he harboured deep doubts about the aristocracy, there was an unspoken strength in Sir Reginald's offer—a promise quietly made but never to be called upon. In that brief exchange, Rory sensed a fragile hope take root, a hope that, perhaps, he would never need to lean on this help, yet was grateful all the same for its presence.

## Chapter 27 - Permission Granted

Rose's heart thrummed with exhilaration as she stepped onto the porch, a joyful pulse that felt like it might open her chest. Her news shimmered like sunlight on water, and the urge to share it with her family quickened her steps. But there, waiting on the veranda, was Rory.

His broad smile was an open invitation to happiness that calmed the flurry of emotions inside her.

'Good day?' he inquired, his tone playful yet warm, igniting a spark of hope.

'The best,' she replied, laughter bubbling forth as she grasped the moment tightly

'I have a trail of three on 6MD.' In that instant, joy surged through her, compelling her to wrap her arms around him, pressing her lips against his in a kiss that tasted of sweet anticipation

It was the start of a new journey for her, and the challenge drew her in.

Rory's breath caught in his throat, surprise lighting up his eyes momentarily

Then, he steadied himself, pulling her gently toward him, his arm resting comfortably around her shoulders

'That calls for a celebration,' he proclaimed, his voice resonating with a newfound camaraderie

Rose felt the warmth of his enthusiasm as he continued, 'I got the green light to bring Albert and Guy home.'

Her heart swelled even further, delighting at the thought of their loved ones reuniting

'That is marvellous, Rory.'

Rose's laughter danced through the open door, a melodic cascade that drew smiles from all. Its clarity lit up the atmosphere like sunlight filtering through leaves, enveloping those around in an embrace of warmth and shared joy. The day sparkled with the radiant glow of unspoken victories, each chuckle weaving a tapestry of delightful camaraderie.

As the festivities unfolded within the warm embrace of the room, a palpable sense of anticipation filled the air. Aunt Rosemary, her eyes twinkling with joy, sat poised at the table alongside Hugh, Emily, and Noel. Everyone clutched their glasses tightly, excitement and nerves flickering across their faces.

Noel broke the momentary silence, his voice steady but imbued with heartfelt emotion.

'To both of you.' He lifted his glass high, his smile radiating genuine pride

'Congratulations.' The words hung briefly in the air, their simplicity underscoring the depth of their meaning.

At his side, Emily beamed, her heart swelling with happiness as she exchanged knowing glances with Hugh

Together, they raised their glasses, immersed in a shared celebration transcending mere formality

The traditional salute felt more profound; it was a bond forged through trials and triumphs, a testament to their collective journey.

Then Emily, her enthusiasm palpable, handed a glass to Rory, whose expression shifted from surprise to resolve

With a deep breath, he lifted his glass with intention, the moment's gravity echoing as he declared, 'To our joint efforts.' A flicker of determination danced in his eyes, and the room seemed to pulse with unspoken promises for the future, their emotions woven together in an intricate tapestry of hope and unity.

'Ah, so when do you plan to begin, Rose?' Aunt Rosemary asked, her curiosity stirring with eagerness and concern.

'There isn't a set schedule just yet; I'll be on next month's roster,' Rose replied, her voice tinged with anticipation, the excitement palpable as it wrapped around her words.

'I'm truly thankful for the chance to dive into this.'

Aunt Rosemary turned her gaze towards Rory and Hugh, her expression a mix of concern and curiosity

'And what about you two?' she asked, her voice gentle but probing

Rory's brow knitted in worry as though the world's weight hung heavily on his shoulders

'I need to concentrate on my crops first,' he said, his tone taut with stress

'I have a lead on Guy; however, Albert..

he was lost in the Battle of Crete

I have to discover where he rests now.' His admission hung like a solemn tide, vulnerability washing over him.

Rose leaned forward, her eyes wide and earnest

'How can we find exactly where he fell during the Battle of Crete?' Determination blossomed within her, a garden of resolve amid the uncertainty.

Aunt Rosemary mulled this over, her fingers tapping lightly against her chin

'A great place to start would be the soldier's military service records

An Australian soldier's record often details deployments and sometimes even the circumstances surrounding their deaths.'

'That's an excellent point!' Hugh interjected, a spark of enthusiasm lighting his face

'Those records can be a treasure trove of context

Plus, the Commonwealth War Graves Commission keeps records that specify where soldiers are buried or commemorated—especially if their final resting place remains unknown

A good number of those who perished in Crete are interred at the Suda Bay War Cemetery,' he added, pride bubbling forth as he revealed, 'I've been researching this.'

'Yes, the CWGC could be a goldmine, particularly for tracing down cemeteries or memorial sites,' Rory added, his excitement growing like a flame in his chest

'If we dive deeper, we might also want to review unit war diaries and operational records.'

'Exactly,' Noel chimed in eagerly, his mind racing

'By tracing the movements of Albert's unit during those pivotal moments, we could zero in on where he might have met his fate.'

Aunt Rosemary nodded, her voice brimming with purpose

'Absolutely

We could even visit local memorials or cemeteries in Crete for a more targeted approach

For instance, the Suda Bay War Cemetery has a commemorated soldiers registry

There may be critical information on-site regarding the battles and where individual soldiers fell.'

'But how will we do that from here?' Rose asked, a thread of worry weaving through her words.

Aunt Rosemary's determination did not falter

'True, but what if we can reach out to families with old letters, diaries, or soldiers who returned from his unit? Soldiers used to detail their locations in their letters home, and families might have received specific updates about their last known whereabouts.'

'Combining these resources could greatly enhance our chances of uncovering where Albert is buried in Crete or pinpointing a close approximation,' Rory mused, his desire for closure ringing clear and true.

'I can gather a lot of this through my job,' Noel offered, his enthusiasm tangible

'With the right resources, we could map out his final movements and identify possible locations where he fell

But I'll need assistance to tie it all together,' he proposed.

'That will be Hugh and me

As the older statesmen here, we've got the time on our hands,' Aunt Rosemary responded with a chuckle, her spirits lifting

At that moment, she felt more than just a visitor; she felt a vital piece of the family puzzle, eager to contribute to their quest.

'Indeed, I am here to assist,' Hugh replied, though his words barely disguised the weight on his mind

Each day served as a fresh reminder of time's relentless march, starkly contrasting with the vigour of his youth.

The labour of mining—once a source of rejuvenation—now resonated as the weary creaks of his joints and the fatigue draped heavily across his shoulders

With every ache, he pondered the fleeting nature of strength

His weathered hands, once symbols of power and agility, now told stories of resilience waning

Deep within him lay a yearning to contribute, to feel helpful in a world all too often blind to the wisdom age offers.

In reaching out to help, he sought not just to fulfil his obligations but to reclaim fleeting moments of purpose in a life waning too swiftly.

'That sounds like a plan,' Rose finalized with a nod of agreement.

'Yes, and I know someone who can assist us on the ground in Crete,' Aunt Rosemary said triumphantly

'Sir Reginald

He had indicated to you, Rory, that if there were anything he could do to help, he would.' Perhaps his intentions weren't exactly aligned with her grand vision, but Aunt Rosemary decided that was a minor detail, hardly worth raising.

As fortune would have it, the heavens opened, showering the parched earth with relentless drops of rain, igniting a spark of joy in the hearts of Rory and Hugh while leaving Rose and Aunt Rosemary utterly astonished, having long since abandoned any hope of witnessing such a phenomenon again.

They stood spellbound on the weathered wooden veranda as the sky unleashed its bounty. Each large raindrop plummeted to the ground, bursting forth clouds of fine, earthy dust that danced in the air before settling quietly. This land was alien to them and starkly contrasted with England, where rain was an almost daily companion.

Enveloped in the rhythm of nature's applause, Hugh and Rory toasted their good fortune with a frosty beer.

'Well, that means seeding is about to commence,' Rory declared, a glimmer of excitement lighting up his eyes as he envisioned the renewal ahead.

'Your enthusiasm will wane; it's been four years since your last,' Hugh replied, his voice tinged with a weariness borne from experience, aware of the relentless toil the seasons demand.

'It feels like a fresh start,' Rory reflected on the weight of his words, which was heavy with longing.

He found himself lost momentarily in memories of days gone by, where laughter and life once filled the air, now replaced by an aching solitude

His mother and brothers had departed, leaving him surrounded by the familiar contours of the land

This landscape stood resolute, unchanged, even as time marched forward, echoing the ghosts of his past.

Hugh raised his glass. 'To a new start. And may the past never be repeated.'


They were leaving. As Aunt Rosemary and Rose stood on the steps, the fading silhouette of the car pulled away, enveloping them in a palpable silence. 'It's hard to fathom that everything is finally falling into place,' Rose whispered, her voice barely above a sigh, as uncertainty clung to her words like morning mist.

Aunt Rosemary was lost in the echo of Hugh's kiss as he departed, and she felt her heart stir with nostalgic warmth. It was as if time had folded back on itself, reconnecting her with her past's vibrant, youthful passion —a past filled with promise and heart-fluttering excitement. She shook her head gently, trying to dispel the wistful thoughts that began to bloom unbidden. How foolish, she chided herself, to still be ensnared by such fanciful daydreams at her age.

'Yes, and if we hold onto that belief, perhaps we can preserve this fleeting joy,' Aunt Rosemary replied, hesitating momentarily as the weight of her emotions settled in her chest. With a deep breath, she turned to retreat inside, her heart a canvas of mixed feelings—hope intertwined with the bittersweet memories of what once was.

Aunt Rosemary approached the breakfast table, her voice bright but edged with an urgency that made the air crackle. 'Do you know what day it is?'

Emily and Rose glanced up from their plates, a flicker of concern flashing between them.

Had she forgotten? The two of them chimed together, a forced cheerfulness in their tone, 'Sunday.'

'Yes, indeed

And what do we do on Sundays?' Aunt Rosemary probed, her eyes glinting with expectation.

Emily hesitated, her voice uncertain as she responded, 'Church.' The word felt alien on her tongue, laden with unspoken doubts.

Surprise etched itself onto Rose's face

After all, since their arrival in Australia, the comforting familiarity of the church had faded from her routine

Memories of hymns and prayers felt like distant echoes, overshadowed by the storm of her past.

'The service begins at ten o'clock, so you both better get ready,' Aunt Rosemary commanded, her tone leaving no room for argument.

A mix of rebellion and turmoil churned within Rose

She longed to voice her dissent, to articulate how the very idea of the church felt like a betrayal to her memories, to all she had endured during the war

But the determined look in her aunt's eyes silenced her

Deep down, Rose grappled with her lost faith; after everything she had witnessed, she often wondered if there was a God to believe in—or if that was merely a comforting illusion

Yet here she was, trapped beneath the weight of expectation, suffocated by the norm.

A glance at Aunt Rosemary extinguished Rose's objections entirely as if tethered by an invisible thread. A tumult of frustration churned within her; this was a journey she had never wished to take.

Yet, beneath the current of dissent, a spark of elation flickered at the sight of Aunt Rosemary's spirit rekindled, a vibrant echo of the past. She felt herself being pulled between the weight of her reluctance and the warmth of her aunt's regained vitality, even as uncertainty gnawed at her thoughts.

As Rose stepped into the church, she felt a new complexity within herself; it was a space that stirred echoes of her past, even in the absence of her faith. The hymns filled her with a bittersweet nostalgia, their familiar melodies wrapping around her like a warm embrace.

Amid the congregation, she found a connection— not just with the joyous strains of song, but with people who welcomed her with open arms: David, Mary, Val, Mel, and so many new faces who sought her company.

Yet, beneath the surface, joy and subtle unrest tugged at her heart. How could she savour these moments of community while grappling with her spiritual emptiness? When Rose returned to Windamere, it was not merely with contentment; she carried a growing awareness that her journey was far from complete, and perhaps there was more to uncover within herself than mere fleeting happiness.

Rose was soon ensnared in a tangled web of memories, her mind drifting back to Aunt Rosemary of yesteryears. Once, her heart had eagerly answered every request, every plea from her beloved Aunt.

But now, a fierce yearning for independence tugged at her spirit, igniting an inner conflict. The chasm between their shared history and her newfound aspirations loomed large, demanding that she grapple with the delicate threads.

'Right, we need to set some rules while the boys are away,' Aunt Rosemary stated, her voice firm yet laced with an undercurrent of goodwill.

'I'll handle the cooking.'

Rose felt a reluctant knot twist in her stomach at this pronouncement. It wasn't merely the assignment of duties that troubled her; it was the unspoken truth that echoed in her mind—this was her home, Windamere, and it felt disheartening not to have a say.

Memories of a similar arrangement with Hugh surfaced, where the unbalanced sharing of chores had become second nature: 'I'll take care of the cleaning.'

'It's a big house, and you have your work.

Let Emily and me handle the bottom section,' Aunt Rosemary proposed, her keen eyes catching the flicker of discomfort on Rose's face

She could sense the turmoil within her niece, that unvoiced yearning for a voice, for control

'I have plenty of time to potter around.'

After a moment's hesitation, Rose sighed, her shoulders relaxing ever so slightly

'Okay, I'll feed the chooks and collect the eggs.' The agreement flowed almost as a concession, yet it felt like a shared truce—a silent acknowledgment of their intertwined lives.

In that moment, they reached an unspoken resolution, two women navigating the complexities of their relationship as they divided the tasks

Each held their private thoughts as they moved forward, bound by a blend of love, duty, and the lingering shadows of their pasts.

As Emily stepped into the familiar yet altered environment, she felt a surge of anxiety mingled with excitement wash over her. The moment's weight pressed heavily upon her chest, and she sat at the table, her fingers nervously tracing the grain of the wood beneath them.

'I want to let you know there's a job coming up at the hospital for an assistant. I would like to apply,' she blurted out, urgency lacing her words. Yet, beneath that urgency lay a gaping chasm of doubt. She hesitated, gathering the bits of her scattered thoughts, before gazing at Aunt Rosemary. 'If you can cope without me...'

Aunt Rosemary's expression shifted as she mulled over the question.

'Yes, I am okay to look after myself,' she replied, her smile warm but tinged with an inscrutable uncertainty

She took Emily's hand, grounding her in that moment

'Dear, it is a great chance to get that new start you have been looking for.'

Emily felt a flicker of hope sparking within her—a longing for independence battling against the fear of being left alone

Her face brightened with a genuine smile, yet it concealed the turmoil beneath

'I will always be here for you, grateful for the start you gave me.' Her heart swelled with gratitude, but the complexity of her emotions—the push and pull between ambition and loyalty—left her feeling vulnerable.

'Go on, write that application

I will check it and give you a letter of recommendation to accompany it.' Aunt Rosemary's encouragement hitched a ride on Emily's apprehension, offering a glimmer of security.

'I will see if I can open a few doors, too,' Rose said

She could sense the underlying worry in her Aunt's voice—an unsteady thread woven through their conversation that hinted at the struggle to maintain independence

In that moment, Emily stood at the crossroads of her aspirations and love, each path enticing yet fraught with unspoken fears.

On Monday morning, Rose was engulfed by fatigue, her mind reeling from the tumult of recent events.

It was time to regain her focus and return to her duties

Just then, Noel strolled in, his infectious smile lighting up the room

'Good morning, Noel

What brings you here today?' Rose asked, curious It felt like he had another life that tethered him to this place.

'I've heard the news—you got the gig,' he replied, his tone filled with enthusiasm

'It's just a three-week trial,' Rose corrected gently, trying to temper his excitement.

'In that case, we'd better roll up our sleeves

We need to get the word out and ensure everyone tunes in to hear you on air,' he asserted, his determination palpable.

At that moment, Rose sensed an underlying motive in Noel's eagerness

He was drawn to Midjal in a way that felt deeper than mere professional interest

'You're banking your future on me,' she stated, meeting his gaze directly.

Noel replied with a playful, lopsided grin, 'I'm hitching my wagon to a rising star.' He paused thoughtfully, continuing, 'I'm joining the Western Mail.'

'Are you relocating to Perth?' Rose asked, her curiosity piqued.

'Yep, I'm going to be part of their editorial team,' Noel said, a grin spreading across his face

'The Western Mail has really made a name for itself, thanks to all the amazing Western Australian writers and artists

I mean, just look at the annual editions! They always showcase the best in art, photography, and literature from local talent

I'm hoping to sneak a few of my own photos in there, too.'

Noel chuckled, feeling a warm sense of camaraderie between them

'You know, the war taught us both a lot,' he said, his voice taking on a serious tone

He spoke about the publication with a kind of respect that made it seem almost sacred

'It started out helping farmers stay informed,' he explained, reflecting on its origins, 'but now it's turned into so much more

It's like a lifeline for people living in remote areas.'

He could almost picture the faces of those who depended on this connection, and it filled him with purpose

'And those sections for women and children? They didn't just get added on—they really became key to keeping the paper afloat.'

Noel's eyes sparkled with excitement and a touch of nostalgia

'I'll be working with this amazing network of contributors, reaching out to readers from rural and urban backgrounds.' Just thinking about diving into that vibrant community made him feel hopeful

'I can't wait to spend some quality time in and around Midjal,' he added quietly, sensing that new beginnings were on the horizon.

Rose chuckled, her laughter breaking through the solemnity. 'I thought we lived in the sticks; I remember you telling Rory he was a 'dirt farmer.'' The memory hung in the air, a playful jab that tugged at their shared past.

Noel joined in her laughter, the camaraderie warming him.

'The war taught us both  what is important.' It was a bittersweet realization but grounded him in what truly mattered now.

Rose's expression turned contemplative

'Mr

Smith, have we changed that much?' she mused, her mind racing back to those earlier days

Just a few months had passed, yet she felt the weight of transformation—both in herself and the world around them

It was remarkable how quickly life could shift, leaving them grappling with what had been and what lay ahead.

Rose turned to Noel, her smile tinged with the weight of their shared memories. 'We should start working soon; there's much to reclaim after the devastation the war has wrought on our lives and this place.'

## Chapter 28 - The Anderson Family Reunited

Aunt Rosemary and Rose stood together on the platform, a quiet tension hanging in the air between them.

The message had arrived just yesterday, heavy with unspoken implications

They were back

No details, no reassurances—just those words that echoed in Rose's mind

'Three months, and they are back,' Rose murmured, a blend of amazement and confusion swirling in her chest

Their return sparked hope, but anxiety lurked beneath
'That is good

It must have gone well,' Aunt Rosemary responded, her gaze fixed intently down the line, searching for the train that would bring them home

Her tone was steady, but Rose could sense how Aunt Rosemary's calm facade barely masked the racing pulse of her heart, revealing her raw vulnerability.
'Maybe,' Rose replied, uncertainty lacing her voice

The sparse letters they had received in those months had been more like echoes than conversations, leaving her restless with questions

All they knew was that they had met with Sir Reginald and learned of Albert's whereabouts, yet even this fragment felt insufficient

Rose's mind was a tumult of hope and fear, drawn towards the faces she had longed for while bracing herself for whatever revelations their return might bring

'Here it comes,' Aunt Rosemary announced, her voice tinged with an uncertainty that made her fingers twitch nervously at her side

A flicker of anxiety crossed her face as she braced herself, the air thick with anticipation and unspoken fears

Suddenly, they were enveloped in the present moment

Rose found herself cradled in Rory's embrace, a brief but poignant reality coalescing around them, while Aunt Rosemary stood lost in a bittersweet memory with Hugh

As the warmth of the kiss lingered, Aunt Rosemary jolted back to awareness

The exhilaration of the platform beneath her feet reminded her of that long-ago moment when they kissed moments before he departed, leaving her with a heart full of love and longing.

Her dishevelled appearance contrasted sharply with Hugh's radiant smile, a grin that seemed to echo with memories of their shared past

'Quite the welcome, wouldn't you say?' he teased, his playful tone barely masking the depth of nostalgic emotion swirling between them

His words gently tugged Rose away from Rory's warmth, like a soft breeze breaking the stillness of a summer day

Their kiss—a rare bloom of intimacy amid the crowd —ignited the air with unspoken longing

Yet, instead of disapproval, the spectators around them beamed, their smiles radiating a sense of shared happiness

The air was thick with joy, a reminder that genuine affection can illuminate even the most ordinary moments

'Let's go home,' Rory murmured, his voice barely rising above the crowd's hum

He wrapped an arm around Rose, the warmth of the gesture offering comfort that belied his swirling thoughts

A sense of urgency tinged his words; he longed for the familiar solace of their shared space, where secrets could spill forth like the evening's fading light

'Yes, we have so much to tell and catch up on,' Hugh agreed, his tone imbued with excitement and apprehension

He felt the weight of Aunt Rosemary's past stories pressing against the edges of his mind, and as he gently guided her off the platform, he couldn't help but worry about the revelations that awaited them at home

Each step was heavy with the unspoken, and he silently prayed they would be ready to face whatever memories lingered just beyond the threshold

'Windamere!' Hugh whispered, his breath catching in his throat as the familiar silhouette of his home emerged from behind the trees

The sun wrapped Windamere in its golden arms, it stood proud and regal, a beacon of ambition amidst the surrounding landscape

The golden rays danced upon its elegant facade, highlighting every intricate detail he had painstakingly crafted

A swell of emotion flooded through him, his heart expanding with pride and longing

This was more than just a house; it embodied his dreams, a testament to what he could achieve

Yet, the shadows of uncertainty loomed still as the final chapter of his aspirations hung delicately in the balance, tantalizingly close yet just out of reach

Or were they? He glanced at Rosemary, who sat stiffly, looking straight ahead.

Hugh and Rosemary sat waiting for Rose and Rory to stash their bags upstairs

'Where to start?' Hugh pondered, the weight of unspoken worries settling heavily on his shoulders

'But where is Emily?' The emptiness of the room around him mirrored the absence of her cheerful presence

'She has a job as a nursing aide at the hospital,' Aunt Rosemary replied, her voice steady but harbouring an undercurrent of concern

Hugh's heart tightened as he asked, 'How are you?' The question felt inadequate, knowing the challenges

Rosemary faced alone.

'Fine, I can look after myself,' she asserted, yet the way her eyes briefly flickered with doubt told a different story

'It is good for Emily to spread her wings

She is far too young to be looking after an old lady like me.' Aunt Rosemary's laughter echoed but carried a hint of forced lightness, revealing her struggles beneath the surface.

'You aren't that old; remember, I am five years older,' Hugh teased, attempting to lighten the mood, though he sensed a shared understanding of their mortality creeping in

'We have years to go.'

'What about the news?' she questioned, her tone shifting as if she sensed a deeper conversation looming, one intertwined with their family ties.

'Let's wait for them to return

I will get some refreshments,' Hugh decided, making his way to the kitchen, though his thoughts lingered on the impending departure.

As Rosemary observed him walk away, a wave of loneliness washed over her

Soon, she would have to return to England, a thought laden with a bittersweet pang

Despite her wide circle of friends, the familiarity and warmth of family grounded her in a way that solitude never could

'Well?' Aunt Rosemary prompted, her voice sharp and direct as if she had little patience for lingering thoughts or emotions

'They are coming home,' Rory replied, a weight lifting from his chest as he spoke

There was a bittersweet reassurance in the fact that they would retrieve the bodies before shipping them back together

It was a grim task, yet one that promised closure. 'That is amazing,' Rose said, a smile breaking across her face as she took Rory's hand

In that moment, he felt the warmth of her touch, a fleeting solace amidst the heavy reality surrounding them. 'No, what is amazing are the strings Sir Reginald pulls to make this all happen,' Hugh interjected, his mind drifting to the dimly lit mines where he had spent long days toiling under a weight far greater than stone

'He was a good boss, a beacon of light in that shadowy place

But his brother? He was the opposite—a true tyrant.' 'Yes, Richard was a nasty piece,' Aunt Rosemary reflected, her eyes clouding with memories that implied deeper scars, not just from the mines but from the bitter clash of familial bonds.

'So when will they be back?' she asked, her gaze turning hopeful yet tinged with anxiety.

'In a couple of months,' Rory said, his voice barely above a whisper, yet it was suffused with an unexpected relief

The first part had gone so well, but as the thought settled in, a flicker of apprehension crossed his mind— what would they face when the bodies returned? Would they be prepared for the weight of memories flooding back?

A small crowd of locals gathered at the platform, their faces etched with solemnity and reverence as they awaited the train's arrival.

This time, however, their anticipation was shadowed by grief; they stood not to welcome home loved ones but to bear witness to a poignant farewell.  A profound silence enveloped the scene as the train rolled to a halt.

Twelve soldiers stepped down, their movements deliberate and purposeful, as they began to unload the draped coffins from the carriage.

Each coffin was draped in the vibrant Australian flag, a poignant tapestry of sacrifice

Topped with a slouch hat that spoke of pride and sacrifice

The air was thick with unspoken sorrow; these men were honoured with a full military funeral, a final tribute to their bravery.

'How beautiful,' Rose whispered, her heart clenching at the sight

The elegant folds of the flags seemed to flutter gently as if embracing the souls they housed

She felt a wave of emotion wash over her—pride mingled with profound loss

'They shall be laid to rest with the dignity afforded to heroes,' Rory whispered next to her, the gravity of his statement hanging in the air like a heavy shroud

He paused, allowing himself to absorb the solemnity of the military presence—their crisp uniforms and upright postures a stark reminder of both respect and the sacrifices made. Yet, beneath his calm exterior, a profound sorrow gnawed at him; the honour was steeped in a heart-wrenching cost.

At that moment, they existed in a cocoon of shared silence, their unspoken grief intertwining with that of the fallen, weaving a tapestry of remembrance that bound their lives forever. The army had meticulously orchestrated every detail of the ceremony, from the timing of their arrival to the solemnity of the burial.

Noel had taken it upon himself to announce their coming in the Western Mail, and his story was a poignant reminder of the senseless deaths in a war for freedom that they would never know.

It ignited a collective spirit in the Midjal community. They gathered in solidarity to bid farewell to two of their own—young men who pulsed with the dreams of a tragically short future.

Aunt Rosemary and Hugh lingered on the veranda, their glasses clinking softly as they sipped their drinks. The air hung heavy with the remnants of an emotionally charged day that had drawn them closer yet left them aching inside.

Hugh gazed into the distance, his mind drifting to his sons, who lay with June. They represented not just family but the lifeblood of his existence—vivid reminders of a warmth he had always coveted but seldom felt. In that ephemeral moment, it felt like they were a complete family, a delicate harmony flourishing in a fragile bubble of hope. Yet, that sense of unity teetered dangerously on the brink of an impending storm.

Beneath their seemingly serene facade lay a haunting truth: they were bound by the chains of their past, each carrying the weighty shadows of grief and regret. The future lurked in the periphery, threatening to unravel the fragile bonds they had fought so hard to weave. With every step forward, they felt the ghosts of their shared history tugging at their hearts, urging them to confront the pain they longed to escape.

Aunt Rosemary shattered the stillness with a voice that echoed with both longing and familiarity. 'It's over; it's time for me to return home,' she said, her words laden with a bittersweet nostalgia that clung to the air like a lingering perfume.

Windamere had transcended mere geography, intertwining itself with her spirit, becoming a refuge far more comforting than Windermere's faded, distant memories in England. Even surrounded by friends England had no family. She felt the gnawing ache of solitude she had stowed away, just out of sight.

'No.' Hugh's voice cut through his swirling emotions with the clarity of a freshly sharpened blade.

The urgency in his tone bore the burden of decades filled with unspoken wishes and hidden hurt

'It took me over forty years to get you here

Now you are staying.' His fierce resolve was a tapestry woven from threads of love and a relentless craving to craft a new story—one where heartache faded beneath the shimmering possibility of joy.

'That is an old story,' she retorted, folding her arms

defensively, memories flickering in her mind like shadows.

'All the more reason to end it,' he replied, gently enclosing her hand

'Rosemary Ashford, will you marry me?'

'Don't be silly.' Rosemary's laughter rang out, bright yet tinged with uncertainty

'We are way too old for this.'

'I won't settle for anything less than a yes this time,' Hugh insisted, his gaze firm, seeking to pierce through the veil of doubt between them.

Rosemary giggled, surprise mingling with long-buried dreams

Marrying Hugh had always been a cherished dream that sat nestled in her heart but never blossomed into reality

They were older now; the passionate fire seemed but a flicker in the cavern of her soul, yet love—the deep, abiding kind—remained steadfast.

'Yes, Hugh Anderson, I will marry you,' she finally murmured.

Hugh exhaled a deep sigh that unfurled like a long-held breath

'At last,' he whispered, his heart swelling with hope and the possibility of a new beginning.

As the sun dipped below the horizon, casting a warm glow over Windamere, Hugh and Rosemary stood hand in hand, feeling the gentle weight of the promise they had just made.

Around them, the whispers of the past mingled with the laughter of family members nearby, echoing the life they had built together.

The spectres of loss would always accompany them, but together, they would weave those threads of grief into a tapestry of new memories.

'Let us celebrate,' Hugh said, a newfound lightness in his voice.

'Today marks more than just a promise; it is the beginning of our journey.'

'Yes,' Rosemary replied, her eyes shimmering with unshed tears of hope. Let us honour their memories and create a future filled with love and laughter.'

As the stars began to twinkle above, they moved towards their loved ones, ready to forge a new path together, their love a beacon for the memories that shaped them.

# Thank You for Reading

If you enjoyed Windamere's Rose, you may wish to continue the journey with the next novel in the Windamere series.

Reader reviews help authors more than you might imagine. If you have a moment, please consider leaving a review.

With thanks,
Barbara Wilson

www.ingramcontent.com/pod-product-compliance
Lightning Source LLC
Chambersburg PA
CBHW012151260626
47155CB00020B/3573